PUFFIN BO

ROUND THE

How do you make a cane toad eat a frog? What happens when Linda copies herself? How do kids get parts in TV shows? What does Rabbit do when he is put on FAST FORWARD? What does it feel like to kiss another teenage actor? Did Pete uneat his meal? How do you write a script?

The answers will send you round the twist. Three short stories and the low down on how the television series was made.

Fact, fiction and fun from the fantastic pen of Paul Jennings.

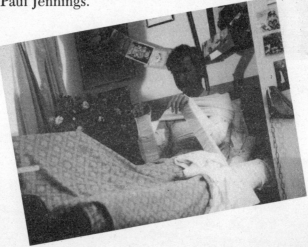

Also by Paul Jennings

Unreal!
Unbelievable!
Quirky Tails
Uncanny!
The Cabbage Patch Fib

ROUND THE TWIST

PAUL JENNINGS

'Writing a T.V. series
was not what
I expected.
Between first draft
and last gasp were
actors, ghosts, sets,
rubbish dumps and
vomited spaghetti.
Here is the story of
the show and
three weird
episodes as well.'

PUFFIN BOOKS

PUFFIN BOOKS

Published by the Penguin Group
27 Wrights Lane, London w8 5tz, England
Viking Penguin Inc., 40 West 23rd Street, New York, New York 10010, USA
Penguin Books Australia Ltd, Ringwood, Victoria, Australia
Penguin Books Canada Ltd, 2801 John Street, Markham, Ontario, Canada l3r 1b4
Penguin Books (NZ) Ltd, 182–190 Wairau Road, Auckland 10, New Zealand

Penguin Books Ltd, Registered Offices: Harmondsworth, Middlesex, England

First published by Penguin Books Australia 1990
First published in Great Britain in Puffin Books 1990
10 9 8 7 6 5 4 3 2 1

Text copyright © Paul Jennings, 1990
Illustrations copyright © Keith McEwan, 1990
Photographs copyright © Australian Children's Television Foundation, 1990
Stills photographs by Greg Noakes
All rights reserved

The moral right of the author and illustrator has been asserted

Made and printed in Great Britain by
Richard Clay Ltd, Bungay, Suffolk

For Julie
who thought of the book

Contents

Danish Pastry

You know what it's like. You stand on the end of the diving board and look down – and you're too scared to jump. The kids are jostling up the ladder behind you. You can't get back. 'What am I doing here?' you say to yourself. 'You idiot.'

You jump. Now it's too late. Nothing can get you back up. You hurtle down towards the water.

That's what I felt like when I said I was going to write the scripts for a television show based on my short stories.

That's what I felt like as I sat and waited for him to come. A man called Esben Storm. The director of most of the episodes and the person who was going to show me how to write scripts. I looked at his photo. There was a blob on his left ear. Was it an earring? Would I like him? Would he like me? What had I let myself in for? And what sort of name was Esben anyway? People in movies are a bit on the wild side, aren't they?

I waited and worried. A car door slammed. I looked out of the window. A man in a leather jacket was walking down the drive. This was it. I had jumped off the diving board. I couldn't go back now.

I spent the next two years working with Esben, writing and making the TV show Round The Twist.

Every script consultation day, Esben would lie back on my lounge and I would sit at the desk writing. We invented characters and places. We wrote new endings for stories.

1

We laughed and worried and argued.

Esben would take my scripts away and edit them. Then he would bring them back. If he didn't like them it was bad news. I had to start all over again.

Some mornings when he arrived he would bring a Danish pastry for morning tea. I finally realised why. When it was bad news and the script wasn't good enough, he brought a Danish pastry to soften me up. The worse the news, the bigger the pastry. I began to look out of the window when he pulled up in the car. How I hated the Danish pastry days.

Well, now the series is in the can. Finished. Maybe you've seen it on TV.

There are four stories here for you to read. 'Second Copy' is a brand new yarn inspired by one of my published short stories. 'Lucky Lips' is a retelling of an earlier story but it has a different ending. 'Spaghetti Pig Out' is also a story from one of my books, retold for television with a few different twists.

The fourth story is the longest. I think I should call it 'Danish Pastry'. It is the story of the writing of the scripts and the making of the television show. It runs right through the book. I hope you like it.

Second Copy

The first thing you want is a story. Right? Okay, well here it is. On the opposite page is a story called 'Second Copy'. You can start it right now if you want.

The left pages all have pictures and bits and pieces about the television show which you can read as you go or skip and come back to later.

There is information about the kids in the show and how they came to be actors. I also show you parts of the various stages of my scripts and tell how I wrote them.

Here's the Twists: Dad, Pete, Linda and Bronson.

Second Copy

Sad, haunting music tinkled down the spiral staircase. It flowed under the door of the green room and filled every cranny of the lighthouse. A saxophone laughed. A clarinet called. A violin wailed. Bronson, Linda and Pete trembled, but they kept climbing.

Linda held a finger to her lips and shushed her little brother, Bronson. She peered through the keyhole and silently twisted the doorknob. The music pulsed and throbbed, sending little electric shocks along the skin of the three kids. Linda nodded and Pete pulled a string with a sudden jerk. A camera flash washed the crack under the door.

'It worked,' whispered Pete. 'Now we'll find out who's in there.'

Bronson looked worried. 'I'd better wait here,' he said. 'I'm only seven.'

Linda and Pete rushed through the door and tumbled into the room. A tripod and camera lay smashed on the floor. On the table a saxophone, clarinet and violin lay covered in the dust of years gone by.

'It didn't work,' said Pete. 'We'll never find out who's been playing that music.'

'This lighthouse gives me the creeps,' said Bronson. 'Weird things keep happening.'

Linda looked around the room, just as she'd looked a dozen times before. 'There's nowhere for anyone to hide,' she said.

THE
SETTING

When I started to write *Round the Twist* I had to think of a setting – somewhere for the family to live. I wanted somewhere unusual. In the end I thought of a lighthouse. It would be terrific to live in a lighthouse.

I rang up the big bosses – Dr Patricia Edgar and Antonia Barnard. They told me they would think about it. Making the interior – the inside set, would be very expensive.

I visited a couple of lighthouses to see what they are like inside. A lighthouse-keeper told me that there are only two lighthouses in the world where the keepers have lived inside. One is in South Australia and the other in Scotland.

In the end the phone call came back. Yes. You can have a lighthouse. I was rapt.

The inside set was made in the studio in Port Melbourne. The outside of the real lighthouse was in Aireys Inlet in Victoria.

Bronson entered nervously. 'What about in there?' he said. He pointed to a tall, three-doored cupboard against the wall.

'It's locked,' said Pete. 'I've tried before. Anyway, that cupboard belongs to Nell. Dad promised her we wouldn't touch anything inside the green room.'

They all looked at each other. Nell lived in the cottage next door. She was old and grumpy but they liked her. Most of the stuff in the top room of the lighthouse belonged to her. She had inherited it from her brother who was once the lighthouse keeper.

Pete pulled on the handle of the cupboard. The door seemed to move forward a fraction. He rattled it vigorously.

'You'll break it,' said Linda.

Pete wasn't listening. 'Something's got to be playing that music,' he said.

Bronson looked out the window at Nell's cottage far below. Her kitchen light glowed palely in the night air. 'Nell'll murder you,' he whispered. 'We're not even supposed to be here.'

'Give us a hand,' said Pete. 'It's moving.'

They grabbed one door handle each and pulled. The whole front of the wardrobe groaned and moved a fraction. 'It's coming,' grunted Linda. 'Pull harder.'

They forgot about Nell. They forgot about the music. There was something about this cupboard. It seemed to beg them to open it. It was like a drink mocking a thirsty traveller.

Suddenly the three doors of the wardrobe skidded forward a fraction. Together. They were joined in a false front. The kids grinned, excited with the promise of a forbidden secret. They pulled harder.

With an unexpected lurch the whole front collapsed, sending the three of them sprawling across the floor. The facade fell heavily across their legs. But they felt nothing.

7

Two clocks are better than one.

What they saw took their breath away.

'Wow,' yelled Bronson.

'What is it?' said Linda.

The middle cupboard contained a fantastic array of old-fashioned lights and dials. Wires and cables snaked between glass valves and levers. The cupboard to the left was labelled 'IN' and the cupboard to the right, 'OUT'.

Pete approached the electric cupboard cautiously. He grasped a lever which was on the front. It had three labels, 'ON', 'OFF' and 'REVERSE'.

'What's it do?' asked Bronson with staring eyes.

They all looked at each other. Pete picked up an old wall clock. He placed it gingerly in the left-hand cupboard under the 'IN' sign.

'Don't,' yelled Bronson.

But he was too late. Pete pulled down the lever and turned the machine on. There was a blinding, orange flash of light, a whir and a hum. Smoke poured from the 'OUT' cupboard.

The fumes thinned and floated towards the ceiling. The kids stared through the drifting curtain trying to see what had happened. Linda saw it first. She gasped. They all stared in silence.

'It's even ticking,' said Pete. He pushed the lever back to its 'OFF' position.

'Another clock,' whispered Bronson.

Linda goggled at the replica produced by the machine. 'An exact copy,' she gasped.

'No,' said Pete as he carefully lifted out the new clock. 'It's a reverse copy. The numbers are backwards. And the hands are moving the wrong way.'

Linda picked up a fierce coconut mask that hung on the wall. It had a large painted wart on the left cheek. She placed the mask in the 'IN' cupboard and pulled the lever. The cupboard smoked and sparked. Murmured and muttered. And then, as before, it produced a reverse

BRAINSTORM

Every story starts with a 'brainstorm'. Just a bit of scribble which is really thinking aloud. When I started it I didn't know what the plot was going to be. I just jotted down anything that came into my head.

'The Copy' was the second last story I wrote for the television series. The shooting for the first episodes had already started. I had one week to come up with a story. I was packing death, I can tell you that.

The Copy - T.V. version

- The Girl says "yes"
- Goes to crankshaft alleys -
- Little man is making clones - fuchsia
                    - works + then fades - pinecone -
- The girl - going out etc.
- Dr. Woolley gone
- Letter - destroy the clones
        - uses it peg.
                    frog
            - blowfly - REVERSE -
            - brooch
            = lots of copies
        - Broken up by bully.
- Copies self
- Go to get bully - run off -
- Copy mentions girl.
- Go home
- In bedroom - food
            - kisses girl
- Fight
- Clone is left.

My 'brainstorm'. Rough, isn't it?

copy. Another mask appeared in the 'Out' compartment. It had a wart on its right cheek.

Bronson's mind ticked over. It thought food. Bronson's mind was nearly always thinking food. 'What if you put a hamburger in?' he said with a lick of his lips.

'Then you'd have a double burger,' answered Linda.

Pete frowned and looked behind him towards the door. 'This thing is powerful,' he said. He picked up the copied mask and put it back in the 'Out' compartment. Then he pushed the lever to 'Reverse'. There was a blinding sheet of light and the copy started to fade. It disappeared before their eyes.

The machine could destroy as well as copy. Its empty compartments seemed to beckon the nervous kids.

Linda shivered. 'This is like a photocopier,' she said. 'It's a cloner. But it works in reverse as well. It could be dangerous.'

'What if you fell in it?' gasped Bronson.

They looked at each other in silence. 'Let's put it back together,' said Linda. 'I think we'd better leave it alone.'

Bronson pulled a face. 'Youse two have both had a shot. It's my turn to copy something.'

'This is really serious,' said Linda. 'Someone could get hurt.'

'Nell'll know how to work it,' said Bronson.

'She'll blow her stack if she finds out we've been in here,' Pete told him. He bent down and started to lift up the doors. Linda helped. They struggled but eventually managed to get the front panel back in place. Bronson watched. And sulked.

Pete looked at Bronson and Linda. 'We have to agree never to touch it again,' he said. 'Does everyone promise?'

The other two nodded their heads gravely. However, Bronson held one hand behind his back. And crossed his fingers.

DAD

When I was in Sydney for a script conference I was invited out to tea to meet Richard Moir who was going to play the part of Dad. I was very nervous about the meeting. I had never met a film star before. He was very pleasant and normal and pretended not to notice when I got Moreton Bay Bugs (cooked crabs) all over my face.

He made a wonderful father in the show and the kids thought he was great in real life.

In the episode 'Without My Pants', the sad bones make Dad cry. Ms James thinks he is crying over the dead mouse and feels sorry for him. Here's Dad with the mouse.

Dad (Richard Moir) is soft-hearted.

They crept out of the room and switched off the light.

Nell looked up from the front porch of her cottage. She frowned as the light died in the top window of the lighthouse.

The only person who didn't know about the cloner was Dad. If he had known, he wouldn't have looked so relaxed. He sat in the lighthouse kitchen and talked cheerily into the phone. 'Okay,' he said. 'I'll see you in half an hour.'

Linda looked up from the game of cards she was playing with Pete. 'Who was that?' she said.

Dad gave his lopsided grin. 'Some kid from your school. A prefect. Hugh someone or other.'

Linda choked. 'Hugh Townsend?'

'Yeah, that's it. He's coming round.'

'Here?' yelled Linda. 'Hugh Townsend is coming here? Now?' She looked down at her grubby tracksuit and rushed up the stairs.

Pete watched scornfully. He knew that Linda was crazy about Hugh Townsend. Even though she was only fourteen and Hugh was a prefect in year twelve with his own car.

Bronson opened the door of their little oven and pulled out his latest cooking creation. A large, lumpy gingerbread man. 'Fantastic,' said Dad. 'You have the makings of a great sculptor, Bronson.'

Bronson smiled hugely. Dad was a very successful sculptor. This was big praise coming from him.

'Smells great,' said Pete. 'How about a bite?'

'Why don't you take it over to Nell?' suggested Dad. 'She's been looking a bit miserable lately.'

Bronson thought about it for a second. 'No way,' he answered. 'This is too good to eat.' He gave the gingerbread man a sniff. Then he said. 'I wish I had two.'

Hugh Townsend arrived not much later. He wanted

NELL

The part of Nell in *Round The Twist* was played by Bunney Brooke. Before each scene was shot she used to walk around 'talking herself' into the part. In one sad scene where she longed to see the ghosts of her relatives she told me that she imagined it was really her mother haunting the lighthouse. She was very convincing in the scene.

In the first drafts of the scripts there was no character called Nell (see my script on page 32). I had an old man named Tom but it was decided that there were too many males in the show, so Nell was created instead.

Nell (Bunney Brooke) knew all the ghostly secrets.

14

something. Dad listened carefully while he sand-papered away at his latest sculpture. An enormous bottom. They both looked up as Linda appeared on the spiral staircase. She wore her best dress. Her hair shone from brushing. She even had on a little lipstick, which was very unusual for her.

She blushed. 'Hello, Hugh,' she said.

'Er, hello . . .' Hugh didn't know her name.

'Linda,' said Pete.

Hugh nodded and continued talking to Dad. 'The winner will be the one who runs up and down the most times,' he said.

Dad looked doubtful. 'I don't know. . .' he mused.

'How will you stop them cheating?' said Pete.

'We'll have marshalls at the top of the lighthouse,' answered Hugh. 'And more marshalls at the . . .' He looked at Dad's sculpture.

'Bottom,' said Dad loudly with a big grin.

A red rash ran up Linda's neck. Dad was always embarrassing them.

Hugh gave a weak smile and continued. 'The runners have to sign a book every lap. There'll be a book at the top of the lighthouse and another one down here. Each kid's got sponsors. Twenty cents a lap. The winner is the one who does most laps in an hour.'

'What's the prize?' asked Pete.

'Straight after the race,' said Hugh. 'The winner gets to go to the footy club presentation night in Melbourne. I'll be going too, of course.'

Dad shook his head. 'Tomorrow's a bit soon. Not much notice.'

'We had everything set for the school oval,' Hugh told him. 'But it's been double booked. The lighthouse would be perfect.'

'Go on, Dad. Say yes,' said Linda eagerly. 'It's for such a good cause.'

15

EXTRA BAD

The *Round The Twist* episodes were the first scripts I had written. I needed some help. The special script consultant and director was Esben Storm. He had lots of good ideas. And some bad ones.

He thought that I should be an 'extra' and feature in the episode called 'Birdsdo'. His idea was that I would be a patient in a hospital who had suffered a seizure while typing.

It was terrible. I couldn't go to the loo. I couldn't scratch. I sat there all day cooking in the bandages.

Esben Storm checks my pulse. He didn't want me to die before I'd finished the scripts.

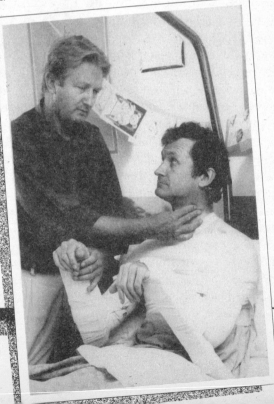

'You've always been so interested in football,' Pete sarcastically.

'I'm going in the race,' she said. 'I've got as go[od] chance as anyone of winning.'

Dad looked at her. 'I didn't know you were much good at running.'

Pete gave her a knowing glance. 'She's not much good at running,' he said. 'But boy can she chase.'

Dad sighed. 'Okay, you can have the race here.'

Linda smiled and looked at Hugh. A trip to Melbourne with him. She was going to win that race.

Bronson hadn't heard anything of this. He was up in the green room at the top of the lighthouse. He stood back and covered his eyes, peeping between his fingers. Light washed the room. The cloner hummed and whirred.

Bronson smiled through the smoke. He stared at the mirror image of his little pocket knife. Now he had two. He turned off the machine and tried to lift the front panel. It was heavy. He struggled, groaned and with a sudden heave managed to push it back in place. Then he crept out of the room. No one knew what he had done. Bronson himself didn't know what he had done. Otherwise he wouldn't have gone anywhere near the terrible cloner.

Pete was next to break his word. Later that night he locked the green room door behind him and pulled away the front of the cloner. Then he took out a ten-dollar note and placed it inside. He pulled the lever and blinked at the blinding light and burning fumes. But he didn't smile at the result. The copy was back-to-front. No one would accept a back-to-front bank note. What a disappointment.

Then he had a brainwave. He put the copy into the 'In' cupboard and pulled the lever. The result was a perfect

Before I wrote the script of 'Second Copy' I was given strict instructions. 'You must feature the lighthouse because the set was so expensive and it has not been used enough.'

I wanted the episode to be about Linda (Tamsin West). She hadn't featured as much as the boys in the series and Tamsin had created a delightful character that I wanted to use more.

Linda and the lighthouse. That's what was needed. That's what I wrote in 'Second Copy'.

Director Mark Lewis (who also made a movie called *Cane Toads*) had a difficult task. He had to create a copy of Tamsin. He also had to organise a race up a lighthouse with only one twist of steps in the studio. Everyone had to keep going up and down the same bit to make it look real.

ten-dollar note. This time he did smile. He was going to
be rich.

The next day was perfect for the race. The sky shone blue
against the lighthouse. Dozens of kids milled around in
their running gear. There was Rabbit, the school tough
guy. And Gribble, the local bully. Tiger Gleeson was
taking bets around the back where the teachers couldn't
see what he was up to. Mr Snapper looked down from his
post high above on the lighthouse balcony. Bronson sold
cool drinks for twenty cents each. Ms James took up her
marshall's post at a table in the kitchen.

'I'd give anything to win,' Linda said to her best friend,
Fiona. 'But I don't have much of a chance.'

Fiona shrugged. 'A football presentation night. Not
much of a prize.'

'A trip with Hugh,' said Linda. 'I'd kill for it.'

Hugh regarded the motley mob of runners. 'Has
everyone signed the book?' he said. There was a lot of
shuffling and murmuring. Feet were scraped. They were
all keen to start.

'Remember,' said Hugh. 'Keep to the left. No pushing.
The winner is the one who does the most "ups and
downs" in an hour. Right. On your marks. Get set. Go.'

The crowd surged forward. Linda was first away. She
darted into the kitchen and up the stairs.

Linda was the first to the top. Just ahead of Tiger
Gleeson and Rabbit. She stumbled onto the balcony and
signed Mr Snapper's book. 'You're the first,' he said.
'Good going, Linda.' She threw him a weary smile and
headed back down the stairs. She was panting. Her chest
hurt.

She kept her lead on the way down and was first to sign
Ms James' book. Her breath came in wheezing gasps.
'Save something for later,' said Ms James. 'You've got a
long way to go.'

'Linda was first away'.

Linda threw a glance at Hugh, who had decided not to run. He lazed in an armchair, staring boredly at the football on television. Linda smiled fondly at the back of his head and lurched back towards the staircase.

She puffed and panted. Behind her came the relentless steps of Tiger, Gribble and Fiona. Linda knew that Fiona was a top athlete and was very fit. She looked behind at her friend and rival. Her side ached. She had a stitch. As Fiona passed her, she hardly noticed the KEEP OUT sign on Pete's door.

Pete wasn't running. He turned the key in his bedroom door as the competitors thundered by outside. Then he looked at the enormous pile of money on his bed. Hundreds of dollars. He rubbed his hands together with glee. The room was filled with his work. Twenty copies of his Zan poster lined the walls. Twin tennis racquets, radios and bedlights stood side by side. The room was littered with mirror copies.

Linda collapsed, gasping outside Bronson's room. A knife-edged pain gripped her side. Each breath was agony. She had run too fast, too soon. She couldn't go on. Other, more measured runners passed her on their way up and down.

Someone else would go on the trip to Melbourne with Hugh. She didn't have a chance. She could hardly stand. She fought for breath. Tears filled her eyes. Gribble looked at her as he ran past. He smirked. 'What a wimp,' he said to himself.

Linda wiped her eyes and crawled into Bronson's bedroom. She didn't want anyone to see her tears. She lay on the floor; defeated, disappointed, desperate.

A shuffle claimed her attention. There was a scratching noise coming from under Bronson's bed. Something or someone was under there. The sound of a living breath reached her straining ears. She pulled back the bedspread. It was Jessie. Bronson's rabbit, Jessie.

LINDA'S
COPY

You might like to compare this bit of script with the page opposite.

Sc. 14. INT. LIGHTHOUSE NELL'S ROOM.   DAY. Sc. 14.

LINDA stares at the silent cloner. She puts the white rabbit inside and switches it on.
The machine activates and an identical rabbit appears. LINDA puts the two rabbits on the floor and impulsively steps into the cloner. The cloner whirrs, smokes and sends out sheets of light then all is still. Smoke hides the view. Slowly a hand emerges from the left door – and the right door. The two hands are synchronised. The two girls stare out, not yet seeing each other – LINDA and her mirror copy ADNIL who has the reversed name on her T-shirt. They slowly poke out their heads and look towards each other. They both scream and duck back. Then they jump out, as one.

LINDA and ADNIL

It worked. I made a copy of myself.

You're the copy.

No I'm not. You are.

They both look at each other, puzzled. Then they point at each other's T-shirts.

▶

22

Linda smiled sadly to herself. Then she picked up Jessie. An idea formed in the back of her mind. She could still win the race. It might just work. But she had to be sure.

She bolted up the stairs to the top room and locked herself in. 'It'll be all right, Jessie,' she said to the twitching rabbit. 'You won't be so lonely after this.'

Her heart beat wildly with anticipation. Normally she wouldn't have taken the risk. Not with a rabbit. Not even with a flea. Jessie would be okay, she told herself. She'd be better off than before. A small voice from within said something different. But Linda squashed it.

It's always easy to lie to yourself.

With trembling fingers she picked up Jessie. The rabbit's heart beat slowly. It was used to being picked up. Linda's heart thumped like a piston. With a sudden rush, she thrust Jessie in the cloner and pulled the lever. She had to find out if it could copy something live.

It could.

In a flash of smoke and light a mirror copy of the rabbit appeared in the right-hand cupboard. It sniffed and then hopped out. It regarded Jessie for a moment and then hopped towards its twin for a closer look.

Linda's brain spun. Her body still ached. Thoughts of Hugh made her stomach churn. She adored him. All reason fled from her. She didn't want to worry about it. She didn't want to listen to the still, sensible voice that told her not to do it.

She wiped her sweaty hands on her T-shirt where the word LINDA was written in large letters. Then, without another thought, she stepped into the cloner and pulled the lever.

For a moment she wasn't there. It was as if she was asleep, twisting, turning in the depths of nothing. And then she felt the blood pulsing in her head. Her ears throbbed. Smoke filled her nostrils. Inside, way down

LINDA and ADNIL
Your name's spelt backwards.

No, yours is.

They both look desperately around the room and see a ship's buoy with ORION written on it. ADNIL'S face falls. She snatches up a book and looks at it.

ADNIL
It's back to front.

LINDA
No. That's proper writing. You're back to front. You're a copy of me. You're the same as me.

ADNIL
Almost . . .

LINDA
You know about . . .

ADNIL
I . . . You, we, want to . . .

LINDA and ADNIL
Win the race and go out with Hugh. I'll tell you what.

They both laugh.

LINDA
I'll run upwards and . . .

ADNIL
I'll run down.

▶

24

deep she felt empty as if part of her had vanished. She seemed able to look into herself and see a dark hole in her mind where something that was once there had left a space.

She stared out at the room. It was the same. But different. Like a dream room. Like the memory of a dead friend which can never quite match the lost reality.

She shook her head and peered out of the cloner door.

Someone else was peering back. From the OUT compartment. In the clearing smoke, a figure moved. It stepped out, just as she stepped out. The figure moved towards her in imitation of her own faltering steps.

The smoke cleared. And Linda looked at herself. She rubbed her eyes. It was what she had wanted. But not what she really expected. There were two Lindas. She couldn't believe it.

Both girls spoke together. They said exactly the same words. It was like listening to two radios tuned in at once. A weird echo as each chorused the words of the other.

'It worked. I made a copy of myself,' they said.

They both thought about this for a second. Stunned. They couldn't take it in.

'You're a copy,' they said as one, pointing at each other simultaneously.

'No I'm not, you are,' they said together.

Each girl stared at the other. Each thought they were the original. It slowly dawned on them that the other knew everything they knew. Linda blushed. So did her copy. This other person knew everything she had ever done. Knew everything she had ever thought. They weren't just twins. They were the same person.

They pointed at each other's T-shirts.

'You're name's spelt backwards,' they said in the same voice.

'No, yours is,' they both replied.

Both girls tried to make sense of it. They shared the

LINDA

And when we win . . .

ADNIL

I'll be on my way with Hugh.

LINDA

You mean I'll be on my way with Hugh.

ADNIL

No need to argue. There's enough Hugh . . .

LINDA

For two.

They laugh and head for the door.

same history. They had both thought the same thoughts. Cried the same tears. Been the same person. But from now on, like twins at birth, they would lead different lives.

The copy looked down and saw ADNIL written across her chest. She didn't seem to realise that it was back-to-front. Linda ran across the room and grabbed an ancient book. She held it out to Adnil.

'It's back-to-front,' said Adnil.

'No,' Linda told her. 'It's normal. It's proper writing. You're a copy of me.'

Adnil tried to grasp it. She shook her head. She knew it was true and yet it couldn't be. She remembered her whole life. She knew about Bronson and Dad and Pete and the race. She was in love with Hugh. She couldn't be a copy. And yet the book, the back-to-front book, told her that she was.

Runners could be heard outside the door, their feet slapping against the concrete stairs.

Adnil shook her head and spoke hesitantly. 'I, you, we, want to . . .'

Linda finished the sentence. 'Win the race and go out with Hugh.' They both laughed and started to lift the cloner door. They forgot all about the rabbits which were out of sight under a table.

'I'll run upwards,' said Linda.

'And I'll run down,' said Adnil.

'And when we win . . .' began Linda.

'I'll be on my way with Hugh,' finished Adnil.

They stopped and looked at each other. Linda hadn't thought of this. Both girls wanted Hugh. Both girls wanted to win the race. Both wanted to go to Melbourne with Hugh.

'No need to argue,' said Linda. 'There's enough Hugh . . .'

'For two,' smiled Adnil.

ADNIL

From the point where Linda meets Adnil, Tamsin had to play two parts – Linda and Adnil. Each scene was filmed twice and then the two joined electronically so that you could see Tamsin talking to herself. She had to talk to a spot marked with tape on the wall and pretend it was Adnil.

For some scenes a double (Jasmine Hirst) was used for Adnil but you never see the double's face. Only her back. This is easier than the electronic merging of two different 'takes'. Here's Tamsin with Jasmine – the girl you never see.

Linda (Tamsin West) and Adnil's stand-in (Jasmine Hirst).

They looked at each other warmly. It was nice to have such a close friend. Without another word they headed for the door.

Mr Snapper raised his eyebrows as Linda rushed up and signed the book. She seemed to have found fresh strength. 'There's seven ahead of you,' he said.

Linda looked confident. 'We'll soon change that,' she told him. Tiger was in front of her. He looked back as Linda put down the pen. She waited until he vanished ahead of her down the twisting stairway. Then she dashed into the top room and shut the door.

Down below, in Linda's room, Adnil looked at her back-to-front watch. She opened the door and rushed down to where Ms James sat at the marshall's table. She scribbled her signature and then scrambled up the stairs past Tiger who had just reached the bottom. Tiger stopped and scratched his head. He was sure Linda had been behind him.

Ms James stared at Adnil's signature. She showed it to Dad. It was written back-to-front.

Mr Snapper looked up in surprise as Linda arrived back at the top. He couldn't believe she had been all the way to the bottom and back in such a short time. He had no way of knowing that Linda had only climbed a few short steps from the top room of the lighthouse. 'That was quick,' he said.

'You haven't seen anything yet,' Linda told him.

The plan worked perfectly. Every five minutes Adnil would rush out of the bottom room and sign Ms James' book. Then Linda would sprint out of the top room and sign for Mr Snapper. They ran easily past the other kids, never getting out of breath. Dad and Ms James stared every time that Adnil spelt Linda's name backwards. They thought she must be suffering from lack of oxygen.

At last it was over. Hugh Townsend blew a whistle and all the competitors filtered down to the kitchen. Bronson

FIRST EFFORT

'I want to write the scripts,' was the first thing I said when I heard that my stories were going to be made into a television show. Then I started to panic. I didn't even know what a script looked like. I went straight out and borrowed one. Then I wrote a draft for an episode and gave it to Esben.

He said it was very good 'for a first effort'. Then he gave it back to me. Everything was crossed out. My heart sank. He had been right through it with a pen. If you look on the next page you can see what it looked like:

▶

did a brisk trade selling lemonade.

Hugh counted the signatures in the marshalls' books. At last he looked up and a hush fell over the crowd. 'The winner of the trip to Melbourne with yours truly is . . . Linda Twist.'

A cheer went up. 'Or should I say,' added Hugh. 'Adnil Twist, who seems to have put her T-shirt on inside out.' Another cheer went up from the crowd. Dad looked at her closely. Something was different. But he couldn't work out what it was.

Adnil stepped forward to accept the trophy. She gave a shy, guilty smile to the crowd who clapped and yelled loudly.

In the top room Linda heard the faint applause that filtered up the stairs. She didn't notice behind her that the clock and its back-to-front copy had begun to melt.

Down below Hugh Townsend started the engine of his old Morris Minor with a belch of smoke. Dad and Adnil were there to see him off. The other runners made their way home in small groups.

'I'll meet you at the station at four, Linda,' Hugh said to Adnil.

'Aren't you going to pick her up?' said Dad.

Hugh shook his handsome head. 'Nah,' he said. 'No time.'

Adnil smiled an adoring smile. Dad stared at her. 'You've parted your hair on the other side, Linda,' he said.

The two girls met in Linda's room. They locked the door and then turned to each other. 'I won,' they both exclaimed together. They laughed and then corrected themselves, 'We won.'

'I can't wait . . .' began Adnil.

'To go with Hugh,' finished Linda.

'I don't know what to wear,' said Adnil.

'Maybe that dress I wore to the disco,' said Linda.

Sc. 5.   INT.   LIGHTHOUSE KITCHEN.   DAY.   Sc. 5.

MR GRIBBLE shows DAD, LINDA, BRONSON MATRON GRIBBLE and
GRIBBLE over the lighthouse. TOM follows along in a
dejected manner. The combined kitchen, dining and
lounge room is on the ground floor. ~~It has~~ W/ windows
overlooking the ocean. ~~There is a fridge, table,
cupboards etc.~~ all ~~with a distinctly~~ nautical feel.
~~The room is cluttered.~~ Glass floats hang from the
ceiling. ~~There are old ropes, lanterns, ropes fishing
rods and a telescope.~~ A spiral staircase leads up from
the rear.

*— the
homethings
have a
distinctly 'cluttered'*

                    BRONSON
        ~~(Wildly excited)~~   Excellent,
        excellent.

                    PETE
        Wow.

                MATRON GRIBBLE
        ~~(sniffing)~~ It needs disinfecting.
        It's been allowed to get into a
        filthy state ~~(she exchanges
        hostile glances with Tom).~~

                                    DAY
Sc. 6.   INT.   LIGHTHOUSE STAIRS.   ~~NIGHT~~.   Sc. 6.

~~The whole group move up the stairs.~~ PETE, LINDA,
BRONSON, and GRIBBLE ~~are in the lead.~~ MR GRIBBLE,
MATRON GRIBBLE DAD and TOM ~~are below them in a separate
group.~~ follow. *⌐hurry up the stairs*
                    BRONSON
        This is my room.
                              empty
PETE and LINDA stare in~~,~~ *to* ~~We see~~ the cell like, ~~empty~~
room with a small window. ~~Gribble is bored.~~

                GRIBBLE JN.
        ~~(Holds out hands in a spooky manner
        and tries to frighten BRONSON with
        his fake, ghost voice)~~. Ned lived
        here. He died on the outside loo.
        When Tom came back, all he found
        was a bleached skeleton still
        sitting on the dunny seat.   They
        say on a windswept night.....
                          to the toilet
                    BRONSON
        ~~(incredulous)~~ I'm not going ~~back
        down there.~~ No way. ~~Never.~~

*Would Pete not respond to
Ned dying on the loo?*

My first script ⌐ with mistakes – for the episode, 'Skeleton on the Dunny'.

Adnil shook her head. 'It's too frilly. I look good in it but it's not right for a football do.'

Linda had always liked that dress. 'It's beautiful, I'm going to wear it,' she said. They argued with each other like someone talking to their reflection in a mirror.

'I'm going in my best jeans,' said Adnil. 'Hugh won't care. It shouldn't make any difference what you wear. Not if he's really nice.'

'He is,' said Linda. 'I've always liked him.'

'I have, haven't I?' Adnil replied.

They smiled, flicked the hair out of their eyes, turned and walked to the wardrobe.

In the top room, unknown to all, the melting clock dripped dreadfully onto the floor.

Dad stopped the old ute at the station. Linda sat next to him in her green dress. Pete and Bronson were squashed in too. Linda tried to distract them while Adnil sneaked out of the back where she had been hiding under a tarpaulin.

Linda looked at her father. 'You couldn't lend me a few dollars could you, Dad?'

Dad opened up his wallet. 'Sorry, I'm out of cash.'

Bronson reached into the depths of a grimy pocket. 'I've got five cents,' he said.

Pete pulled out a fat wallet and handed over a bundle of notes. 'Thanks,' said Linda. They all looked in surprise at Pete's sudden wealth.

'Have a nice time, sweetheart,' Dad called as Linda hurried into the station.

Once they were in the train, Linda and Adnil put the rest of their plan into action. Adnil sat next to Hugh in the carriage while Linda waited in the buffet car. They were going to swap places every quarter of an hour. That way they could share Hugh. He would never know the difference.

Pete loved Fiona. Linda had a crush on Hugh Townsend. Even Bronson got to kiss a little girl ghost in the last episode. But what about poor old Dad? I invented Ms James (Robyn Gibbs), the local school teacher. Dad falls in love with her and chases her through the whole series. I wanted her to accept his proposal in the last episode. Others in the film crew didn't.

In the end it was filmed three ways. She said, 'Yes', 'no' and 'maybe'. As I write this I still don't know which ending they are going to use.

Did Ms James (Robyn Gibbs) accept Dad's proposal?

Adnil looked at him adoringly. Hugh lay back in his seat with his Walkman earphones clamped over his ears. He wore his old runners and a torn tracksuit.

'Isn't the presentation formal?' asked Adnil.

Hugh lifted off one earphone in a bored manner so that he could hear her. 'Who cares?' he said.

A porter arrived. He was young and cocky. 'The buffet is due to open soon, people,' he drawled. 'Delicious railway food. Microwaved pies, hotdogs and coffee. Get 'em before they run away.'

Adnil looked at Hugh. 'We can eat at the presentation,' she said.

Hugh was scornful. 'There's no food there. It's not that sort of do.'

'What about tea?' asked Adnil.

'We'll have to eat on the train,' said Hugh. 'Can you lend me some money?'

Adnil handed over her money. 'Two pies,' said Hugh.

'Self-serve, mate,' said the porter. 'Opening soon.' He winked at Adnil as Hugh put the money in his pocket.

Back at the lighthouse Bronson was very pleased with himself. He was making yet another visit to the cloner. He looked at the copy he had made. It was as good as the original. Nell was going to be very pleased about this. He left the top room of the lighthouse. He also left the cloner switched on. And two rabbits, which sniffed and snuffled under the table. Above them, the two clocks were only melted puddles of plastic and steel.

Nell dozed in her rocking chair. She looked up as Bronson approached. He held out a tray. On it were two gingerbread men. One had a row of currant buttons down the left side. The other had a row down the right side. They were mirror copies.

'I made you a gingerbread man,' said Bronson with a generous smile. 'Which one do you want?'

CASTING

I was tremendously excited when we reached the stage of casting. I was invited along. There were about sixty kids from all over Victoria who had come to the auditions in a huge, empty studio. They were divided into small groups and given scripts to workshop. They had to tell jokes and stories and pretend to be dying.

At one stage they had to come out and tell the camera the biggest lie they had ever told their parents. Boy, were there some whoppers. Most of the stories involved sneaking out to a disco and telling the parents they were somewhere else. Some said they had never told their parents a lie.

The first script they had to read was a scene out of 'The Cabbage Patch Fib' where Pete puts a bit of spaghetti up his nose.

I suddenly felt very moved. I can't describe the feeling. All these people were doing strange things – because of me. I had never heard people act my lines before. It was magic. It sent a shiver up my spine.

'Thank you, Bronson,' said Nell. 'That's very kind of . . .' Her voice trailed away as she looked at the gingerbread men.

She picked one up. 'You've found Tom's cloner,' she said accusingly.

Bronson panicked. 'It's magic,' he said. 'The machine made me do it.'

They looked at the gingerbread men. Their faces seemed slightly twisted as if they were laughing at an evil joke.

In the top room of the lighthouse the two rabbits shuffled into the cloner. And became four. The cloner buzzed and sparked in complaint.

Down below, the gingerbread men melted a little.

On the train, in the buffet, Linda held her hand to her side and winced with pain.

Adnil held her side in pain also. She stumbled along the corridor towards the buffet. The pain eased and she smiled at Linda.

Linda let her hand drop and nodded. It was her turn with Hugh.

'Your go,' said Adnil.

'What's he like?' asked Linda eagerly.

'Very mature,' said Adnil. 'Like old cheese.'

'He's lovely,' said Linda.

'Go see for yourself,' Adnil told her.

Linda slipped into the seat next to Hugh with adoring eyes. 'You've changed your clothes,' he said.

'Those jeans weren't right,' said Linda.

Hugh took off his earphones. 'Did I ever tell you about the time I kicked the winning goal at the finals?' he asked.

'No, you didn't,' said Linda eagerly. 'What happened?'

Back at the lighthouse, Dad stared in horror at the mess in Pete's room. Nell shook her head disbelievingly and

DRAFT HORSE

Esben Storm was a slave driver. I wrote seven drafts of every script before he was happy. Ninety-one drafts in all.

Never in all my life have I worked so hard. By the time I finished I had wasted away to nothing.

Esben Storm and all that was left of me.

then turned to Pete and Bronson. 'Is there anything else?' she asked angrily.

Pete groaned sadly. The money was melting. The posters of Zan dripped down the wall like uncooked pancakes. Everything that he had copied was decaying. And so were the originals. Bronson took out his little pocket knives and dropped them. They were nothing but a gooey mess of cold melted steel.

'None of my brother's inventions worked properly,' said Nell. 'When you copy something the energy from one thing is shared between the two. In the end they both begin to break down. I thought of destroying the machine but I don't know what would happen if I did.'

'Did Linda copy anything?' said Dad urgently. They looked at each other.

'Adnil,' they all yelled.

Adnil was still in the buffet. Linda sat next to Hugh. But she was bored. Hugh had been talking about himself non-stop for ages. He was just getting to the end of another true Hugh story. 'So the principal says to me, "Hugh, this school would be nothing without you." '

Linda looked wearily out of the window. Hugh started on the next yarn. 'Did I ever tell you about the time I saved the whole basketball team from extermination?'

'No,' said Linda. 'But I think you're going to.'

'You've got a sharp tongue,' said Hugh.

'I always say what I think,' said Linda.

Hugh pulled a face. 'When you get to the presentation,' he said. 'Make sure you don't say anything. Leave it up to me.'

'Why?' asked Linda. She rolled her eyes in annoyance.

'We expected a boy to win,' said Hugh. 'A football presentation is no place for a girl.' Linda stood up to leave.

'It would probably be better if you didn't sit too close to me when we get there,' he said to her retreating back.

People told me that script writers are not wanted on 'the set' once shooting starts. They think that the writer might complain if the show doesn't turn out the way they wrote it. Script writers sometimes throw tantrums if their work is changed.

It's no good being like this. The writer just has to accept that everyone concerned will want to be involved. The editor, the producer, the director, the television station, make up, the Art Department – everyone has their own ideas. It's no use getting into a paddy if you don't get everything you want. If you can't compromise, you can't write scripts. It's not like writing books where it's mainly your editor giving you a bit of stick. In films everyone has to have a say.

With so many people pooling their ideas the show can be much improved. The last page of 'Second Copy' has a joke about rabbits. It was the idea of Ralph Strasser, the film editor. I thought it was a great idea and put it in the script.

Linda joined Adnil in the buffet. 'Can you believe that guy?' she said.

Adnil grinned. 'I told you.'

'What a turkey,' said Linda.

'In full flight,' Adnil added.

The porter grinned at the two girls from behind the counter. He thought they were twins. Very nice twins.

Dad was worried. He jammed his foot onto the accelerator of the ute. 'Two Lindas?' said Bronson.

Pete tried to joke. 'One's bad enough,' he said. No one laughed.

'None is much worse,' Dad warned.

'Can't you go faster?' asked Nell.

Dad spun the wheel. 'We'll have to catch them at Gooseneck Gully.'

Hugh stared out of the train window as the sign saying GOOSENECK GULLY slid by. His jaw sagged at what he saw. He pulled down the window and poked out his head. Two identical Lindas stood on the platform. One in jeans and the other in a dress. Hugh stared in amazement. He couldn't take it in. Both girls spoke together. 'Did I ever tell you about the time I . . .'

They laughed, put their thumbs to their noses and blew him a raspberry.

Hugh goggled at them as the train drew away. The two girls put their arms around each other and headed for the ticket box.

'To think I used to follow him around at school,' said Linda.

'I used to wonder about him though,' said Adnil.

Linda smiled. 'I even took secret photos of him. And he turns out to be such . . .'

'A dork,' added Adnil.

'A dag,' put in Linda.

ONE-LINERS

Many of the actors made up lines that weren't in the script. Sometimes we left them in. Frankie J. Holden was very quick with 'one-liners'. In one scene Mr Gribble says to some Arabs, 'You wouldn't give it to your mother-in-law.'

Frankie added his own line to mine. 'Sorry,' he said to the Arabs. 'I should have said mothers-in-law.'

We left it in.

Judith McGrath added something extra in a different way. Her wonderful range of facial expressions brought a new dimension to Matron Gribble.

Frankie J. Holden and Judith McGrath playing Gribble's parents.

'And a total dipstick,' they chorused together.

The two girls exchanged glances. It was good to have someone who understood you so well. Who understood what you were feeling. Who felt what you felt. Who liked what you liked. Linda knew that she would never be the same without Adnil. And she knew that Adnil felt the same about her.

Suddenly both girls doubled over in pain. They held their hands to their sides.

'I've got a terrible pain,' said Adnil.

'Me too,' said Linda. 'Not surprising really. Anyone'd have a pain after sitting next to Hugh Townsend.'

Hugh sat in the train buffet and shook his head. He slurped a double milkshake and took a bite out of a pie.

'Four dollars,' said the porter.

Hugh pulled out his wallet. He gaped and looked helplessly at the porter. His money dripped onto the counter like a hot chocolate bar.

Dad, Pete, Bronson and Nell stared along the Goosneck Gully station. It was deserted. 'We've missed them,' said Dad. 'Let's see if the station master has seen . . .'

'Twins?' suggested Bronson.

The two girls walked silently up the dirt track towards the lighthouse. Linda voiced the thoughts of both of them. 'I'm feeling a bit guilty about . . .'

'Cheating in that race,' finished Adnil.

'We'll have to own up,' said Linda.

Adnil nodded. 'They'll freak out so badly when they find out there are two of us no one'll care about the race.'

They both walked slowly. Neither of them felt well. They hobbled to the front door of the lighthouse and went inside.

There was an envelope in the middle of the kitchen table. On the outside it said, 'LINDA. FOR YOUR EYES ONLY.'

SPECIAL EFFECTS

'How did they do that?' is the question I am most often asked. People are especially keen to know how the cane toad was made to eat all the little frogs in 'Wunderpants'. Of course you are not allowed to feed frogs to a cane toad just for a movie. It would be cruel. So, a small plastic frog was placed in the toad's mouth. The cane toad pulled it out. The film was run backwards and behold, the toad eats the frog.

The little dragon in 'Birdsdo' was beautifully made out of rubber. Dry ice was pumped out of its nostrils to look like smoke. A puppeteer worked the dragon from under the bed. When it broke out of the egg everyone was tense. The square eggs had been specially made and Esben only had two. If anything went wrong, like someone fluffing their lines during the take, there was only one spare. Once that was gone there would be no chance of doing it again. Fortunately everything worked.

Linda picked it up and ripped open the envelope. 'I don't have any secrets from you,' she said.

She began to read the message aloud. It was from Dad. 'The other girl is an unstable copy. You must get her back in the cloner and put it on reverse. If you don't you'll both . . .'

Her voice trailed off. They both looked at the bubbling remains of Bronson's gingerbread men.

The two girls stared at each other without speaking. Without a word Adnil turned and walked towards the staircase.

Linda grabbed her arm. 'No,' she said. 'You can't.'

Adnil shook off her hand. 'One of us has to be reversed or we'll both . . .'

'I'll go,' yelled Linda. 'I've had more life than you.' There were tears in her eyes. She couldn't let Adnil sacrifice herself.

'No you haven't,' said Adnil. 'Everything you've done, I've done. I'm you. And you're me.'

They both glanced up the stairs. Both of them had the same thought. They made a break for it. Climbing. Clambering. Clawing their way up the steps. Both wanting to give themselves up for the other. Neither wanting to be left behind.

But they were equally matched. They both had the same strengths. And the same weaknesses. Neither could get the upper hand. Linda pulled Adnil back. And Adnil pulled Linda back. They cried the same tears. They fought a fight which neither could win. But slowly, between sobs, they struggled up to the room at the top of the twisting staircase.

They crashed through the door and fell onto the floor. The room was filled with hundreds of rabbits. Even as they watched, another four stumbled into the cloner and copied themselves. The cloner fumed and smoked. Electric currents crackled across the dials. The machine

TEARS

The scene opposite, where Adnil dies, is my favourite. It's very sad, but a beautiful moment. Tamsin pulled out every stop for this one. I'm told that she can cry real tears when she's acting.

Even though I wrote it myself, I still feel a tear pricking behind my eyes when I watch this bit on the screen.

When you write a script you are not allowed to tell the actors how to say their lines. If you look at my first script on page 32 you will see that the directions to the actors have been crossed out.

Good actors like the ones in *Round The Twist* interpret the lines themselves and often give them a dimension that the writer hadn't dreamed of.

At first I found this hard to accept. But now that the series is finished I can see that a writer has to allow everyone else to have their own creative contribution.

shook and spluttered under the strain. Another wave of rabbits rushed in. The machine glowed red. It whined a loud protest at the overload. Then it gave an enormous bang and fizzled into silence.

A smoky gloom filled the room. The rabbits started to fade. They disappeared like ghosts in the sunshine. Jessie was left. Alone.

Adnil fell to the floor with a low moan. Linda bent over her, taking her in her arms. 'Don't go,' she sobbed. 'Don't leave me.'

Adnil grew pale. 'I won't be gone,' she whispered. 'I'm you, remember.'

Linda's tears fell onto Adnil. 'I, I . . .' she faltered.

'You don't have to say it,' said Adnil with a painful smile. 'Anyway, it's only like loving yourself. Goodbye.'

Linda choked. 'Sis, don't go. I need you.'

'I'll still be here,' said Adnil. She grew ghostly. Her voice began to fade. 'Come closer,' she said.

Linda bent down, her face close to Adnil's. Her arm crooked around the vanishing girl. 'Whatever you do,' said Adnil, 'Don't marry . . .'

'A dork,' said Linda.

'A dag,' added Adnil.

'Or a total dipstick,' they whispered together.

Adnil faded and vanished like the memory of a dream at dawn. Linda's tears fell through her own crooked arm and splattered onto the floor.

She was still bent there, holding nothing, holding everything, crying for herself, when Dad and the others burst into the room.'

'It's all right,' said Dad, putting his arm around her. 'She wasn't real. Try to forget her.'

Linda looked up. 'I'll never forget her,' she sobbed. 'She'll be there every time I look in the mirror.'

Linda wept in silence. But deep inside, a void had

BRONSON

Every person in a book or a TV show has to have a personality. I had to think up the sorts of things each person was likely to do and say before I wrote the scripts.

I decided to make Bronson love food. He just wouldn't be able to walk past the fridge without opening the door. I also made him into a bit of a wimp. He talked big but always ran away from danger. Still – he was a lot of fun and everyone liked him.

Bronson (Rodney McLennon) inside the set of the lighthouse in Port Melbourne.

gone. Filled by a friend that was no longer there. A part of herself that had now returned.

Many months later, Linda could remember Adnil without tears. Dad had made a sculpture in her memory. It consisted of the coconut mask, bits of the cloner and the statue of the bottom. It even had the hub cap of a Morris Minor welded to it.

The Twist kids gathered around in the kitchen, helping with the finishing touches.

'You should incorporate the rabbit hutch,' said Pete.

'No way,' said Bronson. 'Jessie and Sam need it.'

They all looked up. 'Who's Sam?' said three voices at once.

Bronson looked a bit sheepish. 'A kid gave me another rabbit.'

They all stared at him. 'For nothing,' he added enthusiastically.

'You put a male rabbit in with Jessie?' yelled Dad.

Everyone ran for the stairs. They stopped outside Bronson's room. 'You don't want to go in there, Dad,' said Bronson.

Dad pushed open the door.

The room was filled with a sea of rabbits.

Haunted Places

'How is it,' someone asked me, 'that the kids in Round the Twist *have so many supernatural things happen to them? Magic lipsticks, ghosts, dragons, bird poo bombings, sad bones and tricky underpants.'*

Are there haunted places?

Well, I would have to be truthful and say that I have never seen a ghost. On the other hand, I have been to places that have a certain 'feel' about them because of their history.

I recently visited the Tasmanian 'Shot Tower' where the early transported convicts had to climb an enormous chimney and drop boiling lead down the inside to make ball-shaped bullets. Many of the workers died because of the terrible conditions.

I felt so sad while I was there. I had to get out. The faces of those miserable men seemed to call for help from years gone by.

Round the Twist *is a sort of happy version of this. The lighthouse is haunted. The ghosts play music which calls to Pete, Linda and Bronson. The kids are tuned in to it and constantly try to catch the ghosts. As a result they become embroiled in the supernatural adventures of the light-house and the sad history of the wrecks which lie beneath the waves of Victoria's Shipwreck Coast.*

The next story, 'Lucky Lips', features Pete in a bizarre encounter with a strange tube of lipstick.

This episode is based on the short story, 'Lucky Lips', from my book, Unreal!. The original story featured a mean boy who got his just deserts at the end. I wanted Gribble, the bully, to be the main character in this episode. Esben Storm (script editor for the series) convinced me that it should be Pete. 'Nice kids do stupid things sometimes,' he said. 'It should be about the hero.'

So it is. And Pete's just deserts are a little different to the boy's in my original story.

Lucky Lips

At the casting session, most of the kids were going to go away disappointed. They were all work-shopped together in a big group but we only needed one person for each part. The directors wanted outgoing, vigorous people. They had to look right for the character they would play.

Every hour or so a panel would decide that certain kids were not right for a part. They were told that they could go home. I felt terribly sorry for them. I felt sorry for Esben too. He had to break the sad news.

The kids who were left knew what we were looking for. A girl of fourteen (Linda). A boy to play her twin brother (Pete), a boy who was small and looked about seven (Bronson), a fourteen-year-old romantic interest for Pete (Fiona) and three bullies (Gribble, Rabbit and Tiger).

After a long day, there were only two kids for each part left. They looked at each other, wondering who the competition was.

There were a number of fourteen year olds but only two small boys left, both great actors. They knew they were in the running for the part of Bronson. They both sat well away from each other.

▶

Lucky Lips

The lighthouse slumbered in the sun. Inside, however, Pete's room was gloomy. Pete lay half awake looking at a poster of his favourite rock star – Zan. She sat, dressed in leather, on the seat of a motorbike. Her full lips were slightly parted. A sultry youth leaned against a wall and looked at her in a bored, assured manner.

Pete's eyes closed. His imagination wandered. He was the one looking at Zan. She beckoned him with a crooked finger and pouting mouth. Pete sauntered over and bent down. 'Kiss me,' she whispered.

Pete moistened his lips and bent down. Zan's arm pulled his head forward.

'Pete,' came a loud shout.

The daydream cracked and tinkled to the floor. Linda stood there grinning and brandishing a copy of *Dolly* magazine. 'Did you buy this?' she said.

'Sure,' said Pete sarcastically. 'I was just checking the latest shades of lipstick and eyeshadow.'

'That's funny,' said Linda. 'There's a letter to the agony column and someone's put a pencil mark next to it.'

'So?'

'The letter's from someone in Port Niranda. Someone with the initials PT . . . Pete Twist?'

'There's probably millions of PTs in Port Niranda,' said Pete lamely.

In the end the actors all went home and we voted for the ones we wanted. There was a lot of discussion and argument.

The kids had not only to be good actors. They had to look right together. They had to look like brothers and sisters. They had to match up well with Richard Moir who was going to play Dad.

At the casting workshop boys and girls were paired off. They had to act out a scene from 'Lucky Lips' where Pete kisses Fiona. Each pair had to come out and kiss a total stranger in front of everyone. I really admired them. What guts.

On the following pages are the people who got the parts. I was very happy with the final choices. I asked each of them to tell me what they felt on that fateful day. On the next few pages is what they said:

▶

Linda smelt victory. She started to read. 'Dear Never Been Kissed. Here is my advice. One – take her to a disco. Two – dance wildly for the first hour. Three – dance slow and close for the next hour. Four – walk her home. Five – look into her eyes and if they say 'yes' – kisssssss.'

Pete went red as Linda tossed the magazine onto the bed.

'Good luck, Never Been Kissed,' said Linda. 'And if her name's Fiona you're going to need it. She wouldn't even look at you.'

Pete gave a cocky grin. 'Well, she's going to the disco with me. That must mean something.'

Music blared. Disco lights splashed the dancers' faces with colour. Pete couldn't believe his luck. Fiona, the most beautiful girl in the school, was dancing with him. And tonight he was going to walk her home. He couldn't stop thinking about Step Five. 'Look into her eyes. And if they say "yes" – kisssssss.' He had the five steps written down on the back of his hand.

Pete was already well into Step Two. He danced crazily, pumping his hands up and down like a wild thing. Fiona wore an amused smile as she tried to keep up.

Over against the wall, Gribble and Rabbit watched the dancers. Gribble stared at Linda who was dancing with Jill Henderson. 'Think I'll do that Twist sheila a favour,' smirked Gribble. He wandered out onto the dance floor. 'G'day, desperate,' he said. 'Wanna dance?'

'I'd have to be desperate to dance with you,' snorted Linda.

Tiger Gleeson looked down from the DJ's booth. 'Here's something with a bit more pace for all you rockers,' he said. He turned down the lights and played a smooth, slow number. A few boos came up from the floor. Pete pulled Fiona towards him gently. Step Three. It was working.

DAISY CAMERON (Fiona)

Born 7th March 1974
Student, University High School, Melbourne

'The auditions were scary. After a couple of my friends left, I didn't know anyone. It was the first time I'd been to a workshop and I didn't know what to expect. Yet when I got home I rushed into the house really happy and said, "Even if I don't get a part I had a wonderful day"

'The kissing scene. Now that was interesting. All the couples were paired up and sent to rehearse. It was hilarious watching the couples sit down and make sure there was at least three feet in between them so they couldn't possibly do the kiss at the end of the scene! As you know, lucky me got to do the kiss with Sam in the actual series. It was easier to do the kiss with Sam because the filming had been going on for a while and I felt I knew him a lot more. I guess it was hard trying to do a romantic scene sitting on apple boxes with the tide coming in and the light leaving very rapidly, but we did it and had a bit of a laugh about it.'

Gribble returned to Rabbit. 'Changed me mind about the Twist sheila,' he said.

Rabbit was watching Pete. 'Why would Fiona come with a jerk like Twist?' he said.

Gribble watched jealously. 'Felt sorry for him,' he said. Then he added. 'Twist has had it.'

Pete's big moment finally came. The disco was over. He walked with Fiona through the dark, lonely streets. Neither of them spoke. Pete was nervous. All he could think about was Step Five. He'd never kissed a girl before.

He was so nervous that he didn't see Gribble, Rabbit and Tiger sneaking along behind. They ran from car to car and bush to bush. 'This is it,' said Tiger in an excited whisper. 'He's wetting his lips.'

Fiona looked at Pete and smiled. 'Thank you for a lovely . . .'

'I'll walk you up to the door,' said Pete nervously.

Tiger dug Gribble in the ribs. 'He's trying the old "walk-her-to-the-door tactic",' he said.

Gribble frowned.

'They've reached the door,' said Tiger. 'He's limbering those lips. Puckering in preparation.'

Rabbit punched his hands together gleefully. 'He's going to kiss her, Gribs.'

'Shut up,' growled Gribble.

Fiona opened the front door. 'It was a great night, Pete,' she said. 'Thanks.'

Pete closed his eyes and leaned gently forward. He pursed his moist lips and kissed the closed front door.

Loud hooting and laughing split the darkness. The gang mocked mercilessly from the road. 'Splinter mouth,' yelled Gribble.

'Kissed off,' shouted Rabbit.

'Give up, Twist,' called Gribble. 'No one'd kiss a maggot mouth like you.'

PETE'S
WISH

Fiona (Daisy Cameron). Pete wants a kiss.

Pete hung his head. He blushed with shame. There was nothing he could say.

Pete felt miserable for days afterwards. He didn't want to be with anyone. On Sunday he went to the local show, all on his own. He didn't feel like going to the sideshows. He didn't look at the animals. He walked around the fairground kicking stones and ignoring the laughing kids on the merry-go-rounds and rides.

He wandered between the tents and trucks not looking where he was going. Suddenly he found himself in front of an old caravan. On the side was written:

MADAME FORTUNE
Your Problem Is My Problem

There was a drawing of a hand with an eye in the middle of the palm.

And sitting on the step was the most beautiful girl Pete had ever seen. Her smile was the promise of a gentle spring. It warmed him like the summer sun. Her teeth were as white as the winter snow. Her hair shone with the sheen of spiders' webs on an autumn morning. Pete looked behind him. The smile was for him. She beckoned with a crooked finger and then, drawing a coloured shawl over her head, turned and walked into the caravan.

Pete followed in a daze and peered into the shadowy silences where cobwebs joined hands. At the far end of the van a cooking pot shimmered with a silver liquid. The figure in the shawl turned.

Pete gasped. She had changed. The beautiful girl was now a wrinkled old woman wearing garish red lipstick. She cackled like a monkey squealing in the treetops.

Fear grabbed Pete by the throat. 'Er, I think I'd better be going,' he stammered. 'I forgot to put the cat out.'

Madame Fortune pushed him down onto a velvet seat.

SAM VANDENBERG (Pete)

Born 13th January 1974
Student, St Leonard's College, Brighton

'The audition was nerve racking but quite fun. The
audition for "Lucky Lips" was a bit embarrassing –
having to kiss someone we'd never met before.
People got knocked out one by one at the audition
and I was very nervous. The kissing scene was the
last straw.'

Sam Vandenberg. The kiss at the audition was nothing. His character Pete had to
kiss a pig.

'Not yet,' she chuckled. 'You haven't got what you want.'

'What do I want?'

Madame Fortune puckered her wrinkled lips. 'A kiss,' she said.

Pete stood up. 'Thanks, but no thanks,' he said.

'Not from me, you silly boy. From the girl of your dreams.'

Madame Fortune stirred the silver liquid. Pete's eyes were drawn to it. He couldn't look away. It shimmered and glimmered and then a ghostly figure formed and stared at him as if from the bottom of a pool.

'Fiona,' gasped Pete. 'How did you know about . . .'

'A kiss,' shrieked Madame Fortune. 'A kiss from the girl of your dreams.'

She stirred the liquid again and the image faded.

'In this bath,' she said, 'are washed all the world's grubby longings. I know all. Never Been Kissed,' she hooted. 'Never Been Kissed.'

Pete hung his head again. He didn't need reminding.

Madame Fortune put a gnarled hand into a string bag and drew out a small tube.

'What's that?' said Pete as she waved it under his nose.

'Lipstick. Special lipstick. Invisible lipstick.'

'No way,' said Pete. 'I'm not wearing lipstick.'

Madame Fortune gently pushed him back into the chair. 'It will make Fiona kiss you. It will make any girl kiss you. Just smear it on your lips when you're near a girl and she won't be able to stop herself kissing you.'

Pete shook his head. 'Don't you want a kiss?' asked Madame Fortune. She pointed to the silver liquid. An image formed. Pete saw himself at Fiona's door. He saw the door close in his face. He saw himself with his lips pressed against the cold glass. He shivered as the image faded.

'You can run away from the past,' said the old woman.

RODNEY McLENNAN (Bronson)

Born 25th September 1979
Student, Heathmont East Primary School

'At the auditions I was excited and hopeful. The kissing scene I had to do with a little girl ghost in "Lighthouse Blues" was just as difficult as any other.

'I particularly enjoyed the scene in "Spaghetti Pig Out" where Rabbit vomits up all of the spaghetti. In that scene we were all covered in a disgusting mound of cold and slimy spaghetti that dripped down our clothing.'

Bronson (Rodney McLelland) wearing the ringmaster's clothes in 'Know All'.

64

'But you can't avoid the future.' She put the lipstick in Pete's hand.

'For nothing?' asked Pete.

'For nothing. It's a loan. I'll come for it and get it back at five o'clock on Wednesday. Wherever the lipstick is, I'll find it. If you can't get a kiss by then you miss out.'

Pete took the lipstick doubtfully. 'It won't make the boys kiss me, will it?' he said.

'No. But it will work on any female. Only once though. You'll only get one kiss from each girl with this lipstick.'

Pete put it in his pocket. 'One kiss from Fiona,' he said. 'Will last forever.'

Bronson sat in his little lighthouse room and played with his computer. Outside the sun was setting across the sea. He looked up as Pete came into the room.

'You know that wonderful watch of yours,' said Pete. 'Can you make it beep at exactly 5pm on Friday?'

Bronson picked up the watch. 'Yeah. Why?'

'I have to do something by then,' said Pete. 'Can you lend it to me?'

Bronson fiddled with the watch and handed it over. 'Two dollars,' he said holding out his hand. 'And it'll beep at exactly 5pm.'

Much later Fiona and Linda jogged towards Fiona's house. They stopped outside the gate, puffing. Neither of them knew that Pete was hiding some distance away. As Linda jogged off he took out the lipstick and stared at it. 'Fiona. This is it,' he said to himself. 'Tonight all my dreams come true.' He wound out the lipstick and smeared some of it over his lips. Then he ran across the road. Fiona had gone in.

Pete pursed his lips. 'Fiona,' he whispered. He knocked loudly on the door.

There was a sound of footsteps and the door was

TAMSIN WEST (Linda)

Born 7th March 1974
Student, Presbyterian Ladies' College, Burwood

'The auditions for *Round The Twist* were a lot of fun. But. They got us to tell them why we would be best for the part.

'This is no time for false modesty . . . or any sort of modesty for that matter . . . with people more than willing to explain why they would be the obvious choice for the role.

'We also had to act out the kissing scene in "Lucky Lips". I didn't really mind. You just had to think it was no big deal . . . and it wasn't.'

Linda (Tamsin West) and nose. From the 'Gum Leaf War'.

thrown open. There stood Fiona's mother.

'Is Fiona home?' began Pete.

He stopped. Fiona's mother was staring. Her lips were twitching. She trembled and then tottered forward pulled by an unseen force. She threw her arms around Pete and lowered him in a wild embrace. Their lips met as Pete struggled furiously.

Fiona's father gaped from the door.

The poor woman suddenly stopped kissing. She looked up. 'I'm sorry,' she said. 'I don't know what got into . . .'

Pete furiously wiped away the lipstick. He saw Fiona staring at him accusingly. Fiona's father charged out. Pete ran for it.

'Hey, come back here,' yelled the enraged husband. He turned around to his wife. 'Is there something you want to tell me, dear?' he said.

Things weren't working out well for Pete. But he wasn't about to give up.

The next day at school, the students all filed into a Human Development class. 'Twist kissed Fiona Richmond's mum,' yelled Gribble.

'Desperate,' said Rabbit. 'She must be a least forty years old. No one else would kiss him.'

Pete was embarrassed. He tried to joke his way out of it. 'Women can't resist me,' he said.

Some of the girls groaned. Fiona hadn't come in yet.

'He tried to kiss Fiona and ended up kissing the doorknob,' smirked Gribble.

'Yeah,' added Rabbit.

'You'll see. I've got animal magnetism,' said Pete. He tapered off as Fiona came in and sat down across the aisle. She looked at Pete with a curious expression.

Ms James came in and put her books down. Pete was desperate for a kiss from Fiona. If she kissed him in class those fools would have to stop mocking him. He bent

'The gang' – from left – Cameron Nugent (Tiger), Lachlan Jeffrey (Gribble) and Stuart Atkin (Rabbit).

CAMERON NUGENT (Tiger)

Born 19th December 1974
Student, Salesian College, Chadstone

'The auditions were as I thought they would be only many more people participated. Also, I was surprised at the many unusual acts and statements we had to make under the direction of Esben. Now I know him I expect this sort of thing to be prevalent.

'I didn't have to participate in the kissing.'

down under the desk and smeared on the lipstick.

'Fiona,' said Ms James. 'Would you take this note to Mr Snapper, please?' Fiona took the note and left the room.

Pete looked up. 'Fee oh nah,' he said. His face fell as he saw her empty seat.

The nearest girl was Jill Henderson. She stared at Pete with wide open eyes. Her lips started to twitch. Her fingers trembled. With a look of horror she threw herself onto Pete and kissed him passionately.

Ms James was shocked. 'Jill,' she said. 'What are you doing?'

Tiger grinned. He started to call the action. 'Twist has had a big breakthrough here,' he yelled. 'Jill has jumped him.'

An epidemic swept through the room. All the girls started to twitch and stare. Suddenly in one movement they jumped out of their desks and scrambled for Pete. Like wild, uncaged animals they shrieked and piled on top of him in a wriggling mass. They tore his clothes. They scratched and scrabbled for Pete, wrestling him to the floor.

Each girl kissed him and then staggered away and slumped in her desk. They were stunned. Unbelieving. They didn't know what was happening. The boys stared in amazement.

'The girls are going crazy,' yelled Tiger. 'They're twisted.'

Ms James clung to the edge of her desk. 'Girls. Please,' she yelled.

'Ms James doesn't like this,' yelled Tiger.

Pete struggled to his feet. His clothes were torn. He was cut and bruised. He looked up and saw Linda bearing down on him. 'No,' he yelled.

'His own sister is going for it,' shouted Tiger. 'Yes. His own sister is kissing him.'

Linda kissed Pete wildly and then leapt back and wiped her mouth.

69

STUART ATKIN (Rabbit)

Born 11th July 1973
Student, Glen Waverley High School

'At the rehearsal I was feeling fine. My hands were drowning in sweat, my face had lost all colour. I was virtually oozing with confidence.

'Now the kissing scene was interesting to say the least but I was lucky and only had to do it once. It was still a rather embarrassing thing to do.'

LACHLAN JEFFREY (Gribble)

Born 12th July 1973
Student, Sandringham Secondary College

'The most anxious part of my involvement in *Round The Twist* was the auditions. Waiting all day to find out whether we would stay or be sent home made me extremely nervous.

'It is very hard just to stand there and wait. At any second your name could be called out and you would know that you had missed out after being that close to such a good thing. I was just glad to make it through the day and still be in the running at the end.'

Ms James stared at Pete with wide open eyes. Her lips trembled. She clung to the edge of the desk. But it was no good. The power of the lipstick was too strong. Her fingers slipped from the desk and she lunged forward.

'Ms James does like it,' shrieked Tiger. 'She's going for it. Ms James is sucking face with Twist.'

Ms James kissed Pete long and wildly. Then she jumped back, shocked and upset. Pete furiously wiped his lips and looked up – to see Fiona staring at him through the corridor window. She shook her head in puzzlement.

Jill put her hand up to her throat and screamed. 'I kissed Pete Twist,' she groaned. She rushed out of the room. All the other girls followed, wiping their mouths as if they had just eaten something awful.

'Talk about lucky,' said Rabbit.

'Lucky lips,' yelled Tiger.

Everyone laughed. Except Gribble. He was looking at the lipstick which Pete still held in his hand. 'I want that lipstick,' he said to himself.

The lipstick was spooky.

So was the music that kept coming from Nell's room at the top of the lighthouse. No one could ever find out who was playing it.

Later that night, Dad, Bronson, Pete and Linda stood outside the door at the top of the lighthouse. Dad opened it a fraction. The music grew louder. They burst through the door. Nothing. Silence. The music had stopped. The old clarinet, saxophone and violin lay there covered in dust. They looked at each other and shrugged. The mystery of the music had them stumped.

Linda peered out of the window as Ms James' little Volkswagen pulled up at the foot of the lighthouse.

'Dad, look,' said Linda. 'It's Ms James. You'd better make your move soon. She's a good catch.'

Before the scripts are written a description of every person in the show has to be developed. At first I wanted Dad to be a taxidermist. Nobody except me liked the idea so I dumped it and made him a sculptor instead.

I used my experiences as a parent to develop this character. Dad is probably a bit nicer than I am but there might be some similarities. I once lived alone with my kids on the edge of a wild cliff by the sea just like Dad does. Here are my character notes for Dad:

▶

'I'm not interested in her,' said Dad.

'Not much,' scoffed Linda as they walked down the spiral staircase. 'You blush every time we mention her name.'

Pete looked gloomy. He thought he knew why Ms James was coming.

'She danced with Mr Snapper at the disco the other night,' said Linda.

Dad looked up sharply. 'He's too old for her,' he snapped. He rushed down to the front door with a red face.

'Hello,' said Dad as he opened the door. 'This is a pleasant surprise.'

'We've had some complaints about Pete,' said Ms James. 'Fiona's father says that Pete kissed his wife.'

'No,' said Pete. 'She kissed me.'

'This morning he kissed every girl in the class.'

'They kissed me,' said Pete.

'He kissed Ms James too,' added Linda.

Dad was shocked. 'What?' he gasped. 'What's going on here, Pete?'

Pete slowly pulled the lipstick out of his pocket. 'It's this stuff,' he said. 'You put it on and the girls kiss you.'

'Yuck,' said Bronson. 'Who'd want a rotten old girl kissing them?'

'Stay out of this, son,' said Dad.

'He's after Fiona,' said Linda.

Dad took the lipstick from Pete. Pete didn't want to lose it.

'But, Dad,' he said. 'It has to go back tomorrow.'

'I think I'd better keep this,' Dad said thoughtfully. 'To be on the safe side.' He took Ms James' arm and led her outside. The kids trailed behind.

Dad looked into Ms James eyes earnestly. 'It's hard bringing them up on my own,' he said. 'Pete's getting a bit wild.'

DAD

Poor old Dad. It's a tough life being a single parent. Dad tries to come the heavy with the kids but they can always get around him if they need to. He is privy to some of the mysterious goings on but he is too consumed by his art and chasing Ms James to notice what is going on.

Although his sculptures bring big money in the city they are a bit weird for his country neighbours. Farmers see enough tractor parts as it is. Scavenging at the local tip provides valuable material for his sculptures and embarrassing moments for the kids.

Dad's car stickers don't go down well with the Gribbles who don't want a greenie for a neighbour. Dad knows what they think but he is not about to change for anyone.

Dad is competent. He can turn his hand to most things including welding. He teaches himself to play a set of bagpipes and is wildly enthusiastic about everything he does. He is idealistic and finds the best in other people – this sometimes leads him to some hard-felt lessons.

It is fifteen years since Dad has been on a date. He would like to meet up with a woman to share his life. He makes clumsy advances to Ms James.

On top of all this Dad is struggling to make a new life in a new home. While the sales of his sculptures provide him with a good living he is alone in coping with the three kids who are constantly attracted to the supernatural and are always one jump ahead of him.

'You don't think there's anything in his story about the lipstick then? Something happened at school. Even Linda kissed him.'

'Of course not,' said Dad. 'Look.' He smeared some of the lipstick on his lips.

'Oh no,' yelled Linda. She bolted into the lighthouse and shut the door.

Ms James twitched. Her eyes stared. She tried to resist but she was drawn forward by the power of the lipstick. She threw her arms around Dad and kissed him wildly.

Dad just stood there with his arms hanging down limply. Then he took her in his arms, making the best of it. The kiss went on and on. It was a very long kiss indeed. Nell wandered by carrying a fishing rod. She shook her head. 'In my day,' she grumbled, 'teachers taught reading and writing.'

Dad and Ms James sprung apart.

'Sorry,' trembled Ms James. She stared at Dad with puzzled eyes. 'I, I, didn't mean that.'

'Didn't you?' said Dad. He sounded disappointed.

Ms James turned and rushed off to her car. Dad stared at the lipstick with a devilish smile. He pushed it into the pocket of his overalls.

'What about my lipstick?' complained Pete. 'You've had your kiss.'

'This is too powerful for children to handle,' he said. 'I'll look after it.'

'But, Dad . . .' protested Pete. He was wasting his breath. Dad was already walking off.

That night, when everyone was asleep, Pete crept down the spiral staircase into the kitchen. Dad's overalls lay across a chair. Pete put his hand into the pocket and pulled out the lipstick.

The next morning he left for school before Dad was up. This was his last chance to get a kiss from Fiona.

KISSED OFF

The baddies always miss out on the screen but on the set they have all the fun.

Gribble (Lachlan Jeffrey) misses out on a kiss.

Poor Pete sat alone at the back of the class. All the girls shuffled away from him. Ms James spoke in a loud voice to get their attention.

'You've got the whole afternoon at the agricultural show,' she said. 'Don't even look at a sideshow until you've answered all the questions on your sheet. I want you to pair up. One girl and one boy.'

'I'm not going with Pete Twist,' said Jill.

'Me neither,' said Bessie.

Gribble grinned. 'No girl'll ever go near Twist again,' he leered.

'Not even his own sister,' said Rabbit.

'I'll go with Pete,' said a voice from the back. It was Fiona.

Gribble frowned. 'We'll follow em,' he said to Rabbit.

Pete and Fiona didn't say much as they walked around the showground. Pete noticed that Madame Fortune's caravan was nowhere to be seen. They stopped at a booth where a pretty girl was selling kisses.

Gribble, Rabbit and Tiger were in the queue. 'I'm having fifty kisses,' said Gribble.

Rabbit's mouth fell open. 'That's a hundred bucks, Gribs,' he said.

'Nah,' said Gribble. 'After the first one, she'll be paying me.'

Gribble reached the front of the line. The girl took one look at him and turned over a sign with a smile. It said,

CLOSED

Fiona looked at Pete. 'It's not right,' she said. 'Buying kisses. Kisses should be free. I wouldn't want to be kissed by someone who didn't really like me.'

Pete hung his head. He felt ashamed. 'You're right,' he said. 'Fiona, there's something I want to tell you.' He took out the lipstick.

77

MY DARLING

Pete's problem

Gribble and Rabbit approached. 'Hand over that lipstick,' said Gribble. 'If anyone's going to show Fiona how it works it's going to be me.'

'No way,' yelled Pete. He turned and ran for it. The gang charged after him.

Pete raced through the dodgem cars and ducked behind a fairy-floss stall. The gang pelted after him. Pete looked around for escape. He darted between two tents and into the animal pavilion. The gang stuck to his tail. He couldn't shake them off.

Rabbit leapt forward in a rugby tackle and brought Pete to the ground. Gribble and Tiger piled on top. Pete clutched the lipstick in his fingers. Gribble grabbed his wrist and tried to pull his arm down. The lipstick, like a loaded gun, came closer to Pete's face. Their hands quivered. And then slowly, Pete's arm collapsed. The lipstick smeared across his face and lips.

Pete struggled out and looked around desperately. They were next to the pig pen. He jumped up onto the railings and walked along between the pens. The gang followed. Pete looked down at the horrible pigs below. Their green teeth slobbered with slime. Their teats swung like water-filled rubber gloves.

A keeper yelled out in a loud voice. 'Hey, you kids. Get out of there.' The gang jumped down and ran off. Suddenly Pete slipped. He fell headlong into a stall with three enormous sows. He looked at their drooling faces and remembered Madame Fortune's words. 'It works on any female, female, female...'

The pigs charged over for their kiss.

Later that afternoon, Gribble, Rabbit and Tiger hid behind a bush on the clifftop. They were waiting for someone. 'Here he comes,' whispered Tiger.

A dejected Pete trudged along the track. He was covered in pig dirt and his clothes were torn. He

Madame Fortune (Sheila Florance) shows Pete (Sam Vandenberg) the girl of his dreams.

approached the bush not knowing that it hid the waiting gang.

He looked up startled as the gang jumped out. Rabbit thumped his hand into his palm. 'Hand over that lipstick,' he said. 'Or your're a dead duck.'

'If you don't we'll rip your ears off,' said Gribble.

'Pulverise your brains,' added Rabbit.

The gang moved in. Pete tossed the lipstick over to them. 'You can have it,' he said. 'I've learned my lesson. It's nothing but trouble.'

'Don't give me that,' sneered Gribble. He caught the lipstick. 'Girls, your luck has changed. Gorgeous Gribble is coming for a kiss.'

The three of them ran off along the cliff. They didn't stop until they reached the road. 'Look, Gribs,' said Rabbit.

In the distance a beautiful girl with a shawl around her shoulders walked towards them.

'You're onto a winner here, Gribs,' said Tiger. 'She's beautiful.'

Gribble smeared on some of the lipstick. The girl put the shawl over her head and turned back the other way. The boys ran after her. They tapped her on the shoulder. Gribble puckered up for a kiss. The girl turned around.

She had a gnarled face that carried the wrinkles of a thousand years. It was Madame Fortune. The boys froze. Then they screamed. They turned and ran. Madame Fortune went after them. She shrieked and chuckled. The gang fled for their lives.

Pete walked down to the beach and sat on a rock. He threw stones into the sea. He was miserable, ashamed and lonely. At first he didn't even notice the quiet figure that approached. It was Fiona. She sat down next to him without saying anything. Pete looked at her. His heart thumped. He hoped she couldn't hear it.

'I'm sorry about your mum,' Pete said at last. 'You

BIG MOMENTS

On the page opposite you can read the ending to 'Lucky Lips' as it appeared on the television screen. The original story finished with Pete being kissed by the pig.

Esben suggested that we finish by letting Pete get a real kiss from Fiona. Steve Jodrell, the director of this episode, thought the kiss was too sweet and needed lightening up a bit. He wanted to finish with Madame Fortune chasing the gang. We had big 'discussions' about this.

In the end the director won. The script was changed and Steve shot the kiss, followed by the chase.

Last-minute changes to the script are called Blue Pages. The colour of the paper lets the actors know their lines have been changed.

The finish always has to be a big moment. So does the bit before the commercial breaks. I had to work hard to build up to a peak before the commercials. Otherwise you might flick over to another station and we couldn't have that, could we?

won't believe this but it wasn't me. It was the lipstick.'

Fiona smiled. A warm smile with the promise of spring. 'I do believe you,' she said. 'Linda told me all about it. Look, you idiot. You're never going to have trouble getting kisses. You don't need to steal them. Not you. And anyway, a stolen kiss isn't a kiss at all.'

She gently lifted up Pete's chin and kissed him tenderly on the lips. Pete's head filled with music. It was a long, gentle kiss like winter and spring, autumn and summer all rolled into one.

Suddenly Bronson's watch beeped on Pete's wrist. But he didn't hear it. Nor did he see the gang running for their lives on the cliffs above.

Pigging Out

I have always been fascinated by the things people will do for money. When I was young, a boy put up a large tent in a spare paddock. He dug a hole inside the tent about the size of a bath.

He told everyone that he was going to fill the hole up with water and jump in with all his clothes on. The cost of entry was threepence or an empty lemonade bottle (which you could cash in).

The tent was packed with kids. The boy jumped in the muddy water just as he'd promised and we all went home satisfied. I don't know what his mother said about the wet clothes, but I bet that kid is a millionaire by now.

Tiger's actions, in 'Spaghetti Pig Out', are based on that boy. But he uses a fund-raising venture of a different kind.

The story is changed in some respects from the original one in my book, Uncanny.

There was one section in the short story where a horse let fly with some horse droppings with disastrous results. Esben told me that this scene had to be dropped (so to speak). 'We can't have the second camera unit tied up all day following a horse around focussing on its behind. One blink and you've missed it,' he said.

I had to think of a different joke. You will find my replacement in the part where Dad drops his pants. As is nearly always the case, it's better than the original joke.

Notice in the episode how the different characters'

personalities are true to type. Bronson is preoccupied with food. Dad is still after Ms James. Linda protests about greed. Pete, as always, is embarrassed and tries to joke his way out of things.

Now that I mention it, Esben Storm is always trying to joke his way out of a tight spot. Guess who I based the character of Pete on?

Spaghetti Pig Out

THE YUCK FACTOR

The poor kids in *Round The Twist* suffered a lot. They were covered in all sorts of things. Bird poo, vomit and exploded toad for starters. They had to jump into the water in the middle of winter. Sometimes things were embarrassing.

Linda (Tamsin West) and Pete (Sam Vandenberg) covered in bird poo.

Spaghetti Pig Out

The lighthouse pierced the boiling clouds like a cracking finger. Thunder rolled and rumbled. Rain lashed the coast and savage waves clawed at the rocky cliffs. A bolt of lightning rent the sky and hit the top of the lighthouse with a noise like a mighty oak cracking. The silver bolt seared down the television aerial and scorched its way to the TV set inside. An electric current arced across to the remote control which lay on the floor. It jiggled and fizzed as if alive. And then lay still. Waiting for its first victim.

Tiger Gleeson grinned at his mates, Gribble and Rabbit, from the front of the class. 'Okay, okay, fans,' he said enthusiastically. 'This is what you've all been waiting for. Your big chance to win yourself a great prize and raise some money for the new gym at the same time.'

Mr Snapper stepped up onto the platform with him. 'In principle,' he said, 'I'm opposed to gluttony. But in this case it's a worthy cause.'

Tiger took out his little notebook and looked at his fellow students. 'Who can I put down for the Great Spaghetti Pig Out?'

Linda and Fiona wrinkled their noses. No one answered.

TOUGH
BITS

Here's what some of the kids thought about the more difficult parts of the actor's life:

Daisy
'We were filming the spaghetti scene and there we were having spaghetti artistically draped over our hair and faces. What a laugh. For about three days or more my hair smelled of tomato sauce.'

Tamsin
'It can be a lot of fun when you're actually in front of the cameras but there's plenty of waiting around. If you're not in the next scene or two you may have up to three or four hours to spare. That's when you have to go off to the bus and do school work with the tutor.'

Sam
'I had to stand naked on the back of a ute holding a hubcap over my private parts for a scene in "Wunderpants" '. A busload of schoolkids went past me. At least they waved.'

'Be in it,' said Mr Snapper. 'The prize is a ten-speed bike, generously donated by James Gribble's father.'

Gribble waved his arms like a champion boxer and leered at Pete.

'Come on. Have a go,' said Tiger.

'Someone's got to do the right thing,' said Gribble. He grabbed the arm of his burly mate and held it up. 'Rabbit,' he shouted.

'No one can pig out like you,' grinned Pete.

'I could do you like a dinner,' growled Rabbit.

'Oh yeah,' said Pete. 'Put me down too, Tiger.'

Everyone burst into laughter because Pete was so skinny.

'There's no flyweight division,' sneered Gribble.

Pete was embarrassed. 'There might not be much room in here,' he said patting his stomach. 'But it's what's up top that counts.'

'Yeah,' said Gribble. 'There's plenty of room up there.'

Everyone laughed again.

'It's a disgraceful waste of food,' said Linda. 'I'm calling a boycott.'

'Don't you mean girlcott,' jeered Rabbit.

'It's only a bit of fun,' said Mr Snapper. 'A show. For a good cause. Come on, we need two more volunteers.'

'I'd do it myself,' said Tiger. 'But I'm on doctor's orders to rest my mouth.' He ducked as someone threw a rolled up piece of paper at him.

Two girls put up their hands. Bessie and Tanya. Pete smiled to himself. If he put in enough practice he reckoned he had a chance of winning that bike.

Dad was working on a new form of sculpture when the kids arrived home. He had a flat piece of wood laid out on the floor. He tipped cans of spaghetti, baked beans and corn flakes onto it. He stirred it with a stick. The kids

**SUCKED
IN**

Stuart

'Filming "The Spaghetti Pig Out" was not the most enjoyable thing I have done. Eating bowl after bowl of cold, congealed spaghetti was not my idea of fun and I was glad when it was all over.'

tramped past it without comment. They headed straight for the fridge.

'It's not fair,' said Bronson. 'They won't let me enter the Pig Out.'

Linda gave him a smile. 'That's because you're a professional.'

'No one else would stand a chance,' said Pete.

'Hi, kids,' said Dad. 'What did you do at school today?'

'Nothing,' said Bronson. He looked at Pete. 'I'm going to be your coach. Nobody knows more about food than me,' he said as he took a bite out of an enormous piece of cake.

Nell's cat Bad Smell walked across the food sculpture and sniffed it. 'Get off,' said Dad. He tossed Bad Smell onto the sofa. Her foot hit the FAST FORWARD button on the remote control. A green laser beam shot out and zapped a fly on the wall.

The fly screamed around the room like a jet fighter. The noise was piercing. Dad and the kids all watched it with interest.

'I got this book out of the library,' said Bronson. '*The Guinness Book of Records*. A man ate seventy pies in two hours. A world record.'

'I could never fit all that in,' said Pete.

The fly spatted through the lighthouse window like a tiny bullet. Dad frowned and looked at the kids. No one was sure what had happened.

'Come on,' said Pete to Bronson. 'We're going to do a little spying.'

The two boys made their way down to Rabbit's Barn. They crept inside and peeped over some hay bales. Rabbit lay on his back on the dirt floor. On a fire, a pot of spaghetti bubbled and gurgled. Empty food cans were everywhere.

Gribble held a huge forkful of spaghetti and meat sauce. 'Come on, bubbies,' he said. 'Open up the hangar

93

VOMIT

Some people were worried when they read the spaghetti-vomit scene. 'Paul,' I was asked, 'There won't be too much vomit will there? Just a little spray to give the suggestion. We mustn't overdo it.'

'No,' I cried. 'Truckloads. Everyone has to be covered in it.'

The producer, Antonia Barnard, entered the discussion. 'We can't afford truckloads,' she said.

If you look at the next photo and the one in the colour section you'll see what I got (or should I say what the kids got).

and let the aeroplane in.'

Rabbit groaned. His face was smeared in meat sauce. Spaghetti ends dribbled from his mouth like a wet mop. He chewed slowly, groaning and holding his stomach. Tiger massaged his cheeks. 'Come on,' he said. 'You can do it. The eighth plate.'

A rumbling noise came from Rabbit's stomach. 'Don't throw up,' yelled Tiger excitedly. 'It's against the rules. You lose if you spew.'

'Eight plates,' Pete whispered from his hiding place. 'It's enough to make you sick.' He crept silently out of the barn followed by Bronson.

'You have to train,' said Bronson. 'Starting today.'

Only Bronson could have dreamed up such a weird training program. He looked up to the top of the lighthouse and shouted through a megaphone. 'Faster, go, go, go. Move those jaws. Move those jaws.'

Bronson's watch beeped. 'Three metres in five minutes. Not fast enough.'

Far above, Pete leaned over the lighthouse railing. From his mouth dangled an enormous length of spaghetti. Thirty metres, knotted into a single strand, stretched from the railing to the ground. Pete chewed slowly. His jaw ached. The spaghetti inched up.

'What's that crazy boy doing now?' said a voice.

Bronson turned round and saw Nell. 'Chewing training,' enthused Bronson. 'We're working on swallowing skills.'

Suddenly Pete's face grew alarmed. He turned and looked behind him. Sad, haunting music came from Nell's room behind him. It made a shiver run up his spine. The piece of spaghetti fell from his mouth. It dropped like a wet string, right into the end of Bronson's megaphone.

Bronson pointed the megaphone at Nell's ear. 'How

RABBIT
SPEW

Bronson (Rodney McLennan) cops the spaghetti vomit.

come music comes out of that empty room?' he boomed.

Nell held a hand against her ear and shook her head with pain. She gave Bronson a dirty look and stamped off without answering.

Pete didn't feel like anything to eat that night. But Linda did. 'I'm starving,' she said as she opened the fridge.

'What's for tea?' asked Bronson hungrily.

'I thought I might take you out to that new spaghetti bar in town,' said Dad.

'Oh no,' groaned Pete. He flopped onto the sofa and picked up the remote control. He pointed at the TV set and pressed the PLAY button. A small, green spark zapped across the room and hit the television. Pete frowned. He pressed the PAUSE button without looking at where he was pointing.

Another green spark pinged across the room. It hit Bad Smell fair in the face. Bad Smell froze solid. Not moving. Not blinking. Not even breathing. Pete's jaw sagged.

Bronson spotted Bad Smell, standing there stiff and solid. 'Bad Smell, speak to me,' he yelled.

Dad picked up the cat and turned it upside down. Its legs pointed to the ceiling. Dad held Bad Smell to his ear. 'I'm sorry,' he said. 'But I'm afraid she's gone.'

Bronson's eyes filled with tears. 'What happened?'

Pete shook his head and pretended not to know.

'I'll have to tell Nell,' said Dad. 'It's her cat.' He put Bad Smell down and went out of the door.

'It's this thing,' yelled Pete. 'It pings. It hit Bad Smell.'

'Give it to me,' said Bronson. He grabbed the control and pressed PLAY. A green flash shot across the room. Bad Smell opened an eye and began to purr as if nothing had happened.

'She's alive,' whispered Linda in delight. They crowded round the cat, patting and stroking it in disbelief. Bronson fiddled with the control. He pressed

There are many stages in writing a script. The first is called a short storyline. It tells the whole story in one paragraph.

Here's my short storyline for 'Spaghetti Pig Out':

> ### SPAGHETTI PIG OUT
> Dad's video player is not what it seems. The remote control unit works on people. The PAUSE button freezes everyone. The FAST FORWARD gives real meaning to an instant meal. But it is the REWIND that causes most trouble. Especially when Gribble pigs out in a spaghetti-eating competition and feels a little sick as a result.

The short storylines are used to sell the show to the television stations. If anyone is interested in buying the show, the writing is taken up to first draft of the script stage.

But things can go wrong. People may be interested but then back out later. When I became involved I didn't realise that most scripts are never made into films. They have to be sold first. I don't think I would have started if I had known all of that writing might have been for nothing.

PAUSE. Nobody noticed the green zap that hit Linda in the chest. She stood there, solid, silent, with one arm raised as if she was holding a flag.

Nell and Dad rushed into the room. 'She just keeled over,' Dad said. 'And. . .' They both looked at the cat. Bad Smell was busy washing herself.

'What do you mean, dead?' growled Nell. 'Look at it.' She picked up Bad Smell and stormed off.

Dad rushed out after her. 'Its heart had stopped beating,' he mumbled. 'Something peculiar. . .' His voice trailed off.

Pete glanced at the control in Bronson's hand. 'Give it back,' he ordered. Bronson didn't want to. Pete dived on him and they wrestled for it. They bumped into Linda who fell like a tree toppling. She lay on the floor with her arm still raised. Her glassy eyes stared straight ahead.

Bronson and Pete stared at her with wide open eyes. They stared at each other guiltily. 'Look what you've done,' gasped Bronson.

With shaking hands Bronson pointed the control at Linda and pressed PLAY. Her eyes flashed. She gave a judo cry and rushed at Bronson. Without thinking he zapped her with the SLOW button. Linda moved as if her limbs were made of lead. She travelled forward in slow motion. She lumbered on slowly, smoothly, with a long, drawn-out cry. Bronson stepped to one side and zapped her with PLAY. She rushed forward and crashed into the wall.

The kids all looked at each other – amazed. 'This thing's powerful,' said Pete. He looked out of the window to the shed. Dad was doing some work on a steel sculpture with an oxy torch. A large bronze figure swung from the roof by a steel cable.

The kids looked at each other wickedly. They crept outside to the shed and peered through the window. Pete pointed the control at Dad and pressed PAUSE. They all

This is the next step. The long storyline gives a bit more detail. Here is my long storyline for 'Spaghetti Pig Out':

EPISODE 6: SPAGHETTI PIG OUT

Episode Title Tag: A plateful of spaghetti starts to twirl and move of its own accord. It spells out the words SPAGHETTI PIG OUT.

* * * * * * *

Pete is keen to make a big impression on Fiona and decides that he should enter a spaghetti eating competition at school. The first prize is a Honda scramble bike. Gribble has also entered the competition and boasts that he is going to win.

When Dad arrives home he has a surprise for the kids. It is a video player, the likes of which has never been seen before. It is shaped like a cake and seems to be made out of a spongy substance. Dad bought it cheap from a bloke in the pub. It has a remote control with buttons that resemble licorice blocks. 'Pathetic,' says Linda. She and Bronson go off to cook tea.

Pete finds that when he accidentally presses

▶

giggled as Dad stood there frozen. The flame from the oxy torch continued to burn. Dad didn't move. The bronze statue swung from the roof. Each time it swung, the steel cable moved through the bright blue flame.

A car door slammed behind the kids. It was Ms James. If Dad had known that she was there he would have blushed. And rushed to meet her. But Dad didn't know anything. He stood there, stiller than the statue which swung above him.

The kids ducked behind a bush to see what would happen.

Ms James approached Dad from behind. 'Tony, Tony,' she said. There was no answer.

'I've got some tickets for the Capitol tomorrow,' she went on. Dad stood silently welding. The cable swung and passed through the flame. It was half burnt through. 'And then afterwards I thought you might like a little supper at my place.' There was no answer.

The kids grinned. Supper afterwards. Dad would certainly like that.

'Tony, Tony. All right, be like that. Ralph Snapper might like to come if you're not interested.'

The bronze statue suddenly fell. A projecting arm hooked the belt of Dad's trousers and pulled them down. Ms James jumped back in alarm and then smiled. Dad still stood there frozen, with his pants around his ankles.

Linda took the control from Pete and pressed PLAY. Dad turned and saw Ms James. Then he looked at his pants. A red blush swept over his face. He grabbed his pants and pulled them up with an embarrassed grin.

Linda just couldn't resist it. She pointed the control and pressed REPEAT. Dad whipped his pants down. Then up. Then down. Up, down, up, down, up, down. Ms James frowned in nervous bewilderment as Dad pulled his pants up and down in front of her. Linda pressed PLAY and a little green spark hit Dad. He stopped and stared at

one of the remote control buttons it 'pauses'
Shovel the dog. Pete can't believe it.
When he presses PLAY Shovel unfreezes and goes
on as usual. The FAST FORWARD button works on
a fly in the same way. The fly goes into fast
forward and disappears. Pete can hear it
screaming around the room.

The other three are eating tea. Pete points the
remote control at them and presses PAUSE. Dad,
Linda and Bron freeze like statues with the food
half way up to their mouths. Pete gives Dad a
push and he topples over, stiff as a board. When
he 'unpauses' them, Dad, Linda and Pete can't
figure out what has happened. Pete decides to
keep his find a secret.

The next day is Sunday. Pete walks into town
to try and find Fiona and impress her with the
remote control unit. He sees a man eating in a
cafe. He presses REWIND and the man starts
uneating his food. He puts his fork up to his
mouth and places the food back on the plate
where it reforms. Pete quickly presses PLAY and
the man starts re-eating his meal. The customers
squeal in horror and surprise.

Gribble and Rabbit have seen the whole thing.
They grab the remote control. Pete tries to get it

▶

Ms James with his mouth hanging open.

The kids rushed into the shed.

'Is your Dad all right?' asked Ms James.

'He's been repeating himself a bit lately,' said Pete.

That night Mr Gribble and his wife, Matron Gribble, were having tea in the new spaghetti bar. They preferred not to sit with their son who was at another table with his mates. Gribble and Tiger were coaching Rabbit as he shovelled in an enormous bowl of spaghetti. 'Go, go, go, you little beauty. You can't lose,' said Gribble.

Dad and the kids walked in and headed for an empty table. Mr Gribble leaned over and tugged Dad's sleeve. Dad stopped. 'Grab that table,' he said to the kids.

'Ah, Tony,' said Mr Gribble. 'Have you thought about my offer? It's more than generous.'

'We're not selling the lighthouse, Harold,' said Dad firmly. He tried to get away but Mr Gribble held his arm.

The kids sat down at their table and examined the remote control. 'This could be very useful,' said Pete.

Linda nodded. 'We should make a pact never to use it on each other again.'

'Who can we use it on?' asked Bronson.

At that moment Gribble and his gang approached from behind. 'What's this?' said Gribble. He leaned over and snatched the remote control from Pete's hand.

Pete dived frantically. 'Give that back,' he yelled. Gribble held the control up in the air. His finger pressed the button marked REWIND. A green flash shot across the room. And hit Mr Gribble.

The poor man started to uneat his meal. He lifted his fork to his mouth and took out bits of egg and sausage and put them back on the plate. The food slid around on the plate and formed itself into a whole sausage and egg. Mr Gribble unsipped his coffee. He lifted the cup to his lips and spat little squirts back into the cup until it was full.

103

back but they put him on PAUSE and run away. He is frozen on the footpath. Fiona thinks he is playing the fool and storms off in a huff.

After a bit the pause effect wears off. Pete wants his remote control back. He sees Linda on a horse and jumps up behind her. They gallop off in pursuit of Gribble and Rabbit who are in a queue to get into the footy. Gribble points the control at Pete, Linda and the horse (who has just let fly with some droppings). Pete screams as Gribble presses REWIND. The horse and its passengers gallop backwards and the droppings return from whence they came. Then Gribble puts them all on PAUSE and disappears. Once again the pause effect lasts only for a few minutes.

The following day Pete finds himself on the stage in front of the whole school. He has plates and plates of spaghetti in front of him. Gribble and two other finalists are next to him.

'The winner will be the one who eats the most plates in fifteen minutes,' announces Snapper.

Pete can see Fiona looking at him from the front row. He can also see Rabbit sitting further along with the control. He realises that Rabbit will probably put him into REVERSE once the competition starts and make him uneat all his bowls of spaghetti so that he will lose the competition and appear a fool in front of Fiona. Pete groans in despair.

Matron Gribble couldn't believe what she was seeing. Her eyes widened. Her jaw dropped. 'Stop playing with your food,' she snapped.

Gribble looked at his father. Then at the control. 'Press PLAY,' whispered Pete. Gribble pointed the control and did as Pete said. He rezapped his father. Mr Gribble immediately started to eat his meal all over again. He drank his coffee for the second time.

Tiger stared at the control with wide open eyes. 'We're onto something here, Gribs,' he said.

'Give that back,' yelled Pete desperately.

Gribble gave a horrible leer and checked to see that the adults weren't watching. 'Later, Twist. Later,' he leered.

Pete jumped up. But stopped. Gribble was pointing the control straight at him. The gang rushed out of the cafe and disappeared down the street.

Pete, Linda and Bronson couldn't sleep that night. They worried about what Gribble was going to do with the control. The next day was Monday. A school day. They shuddered to think what he might do to them. They were so nervous that they had no time to think about the Spaghetti Pig Out on Tuesday.

Monday finally came. Linda peered out of the bus window as it pulled up at the school. 'They weren't on the bus,' she said. 'Maybe they're not here.'

Bronson smiled cheerfully. 'They must be sick. We're saved,' he said.

Pete shook his head. 'Don't bet on it. Now Gribble's got the control I've had it. He'll be waiting for me at school.'

'What are you going to do?' asked Linda.

Pete gave her a wink and took something out of his pocket. 'I've got a secret weapon.' He showed her a small hand mirror.

SCENE BREAKDOWNS

Next come the scene breakdowns. The writer has to explain everything that will be in each scene.

I had to try to make it sound interesting because the producers were now using my scene breakdowns to try and sell the show.

Here is part of one scene breakdown out of 'Spaghetti Pig Out'. As you can see, it is different to the final version because I replaced this scene breakdown with the joke about Dad's pants falling down.

13. INT. LIGHTHOUSE STAIRS. DAY.

Pete and Linda race down the steps.

Dad still sits frozen, the flame eating away into the pole. The top of the pole bends over. It is going to fall on Dad.

Pete and Linda burst out of the lighthouse door. They see the sagging pole. Linda pushes furiously at the buttons. She hits PLAY. Dad comes to life. He looks up and jumps out of the way just as the pole crashes to the ground. He picks himself up, baffled. 'What happened?' he says. Linda opens her mouth to tell him but Pete interrupts. 'The sculpture has a life of its own,' he says. Dad stands back and looks at his work. 'I like it,' he says. 'It looks better than before.'

The kids jumped off the bus and looked around worriedly. 'No sign of them,' said Pete. He didn't notice the bus go flying off backwards down the road and round the corner.

'Maybe Gribble has frozen himself for ever,' said Bronson hopefully.

'No such luck,' said Pete. 'The control only works for a while, then everything goes back to normal.'

'Think what he could do with it,' said Linda. Behind her a girl stood frozen, reaching up at the netball hoop. A basketball floated without moving above the hoop.

Bronson was deep in thought. 'I wouldn't like to be in Gribble's bad books. What if he froze you while you were having a sh. . .'

'Bronson,' yelled Linda indignantly.

'Shower, I was going to say shower,' said Bronson.

They walked on without seeing the small, immobile dog that was welded solid to a tree by a stream of a petrified pee.

'He wouldn't use it on little kids, would he?' said Bronson.

A small girl skipped at a furious rate behind them. She moved so fast that her legs were an invisible blur. The rope whirred like a propeller. The kids went into the school without even seeing her. They also failed to notice the gardener who was digging at lightning speed. Dirt flew like fury. He was already up to his knees in a hole.

The first class was music – one of Mr Snapper's subjects. Everyone was lined up like a choir with the school band on one side. Mr Snapper waved his hands around theatrically and the students started singing 'Click Go the Shears'.

Pete could see Gribble, Rabbit and Tiger sniggering. Suddenly, a big kid who was playing the trombone started to play like crazy. He went faster and faster. No one could keep up. His trombone slide moved so quickly

AD
LIBBING

Tiger (Cameron Nugent) is a character who partly created himself.

At the casting session Cameron was one of 'the gang'. They were doing a scene where Pete has to put his hand into a box and pull out the contents. It was called 'Gribble's Nerve Test'.

Esben was casting. 'Call the action,' he said to Cameron. 'Don't just stand there looking.'

Cameron obliged. He was fantastic. He called the action as if it was a horse race. He made things up. We decided on the spot that he would be Tiger.

Tiger ended up calling the 'Spaghetti Pig Out', the frog race, Pete's kiss, and the school disco. What was originally a very small part suddenly became much bigger. All because Cameron put in the extra effort.

that it was invisible. Smoke started to pour out of the instrument. Suddenly the trombonist stopped and dropped the smouldering instrument in amazement. He shook his burnt hand and hopped up and down.

'Stop showing off, Henderson,' said Mr Snapper. 'There is no place here for exhibitionists. Stay with the others.'

The band struck up again. Pete kept a close eye on Gribble. He saw his enemy reach into his pocket. And take out the control. Without warning he zapped Mr Snapper with FAST FORWARD. Mr Snapper started conducting furiously. His hands flew. The band and singers tried to keep up. Faster and faster they sang. They finished one verse in ten seconds.

Finally everyone collapsed, exhausted. They thought it was a great joke. Poor Mr Snapper kept going. Flat out.

Gribble pointed the control at Linda. But a hand reached down and grabbed it. It was Pete.

'Thief,' yelled Gribble. Pete bolted out of the door.

'You're gone, Twist,' said Rabbit. He thumped one hand into another and then raced off after Pete. Gribble followed.

'And they're racing,' said Tiger. He ran after them, calling the action as he went.

Pete fled down the corridor, turning and firing at the gang. Green sparks bounced off the floor and walls. He narrowly missed the school librarian who tottered along with a high stack of books.

Rabbit ducked as Pete fired at him. The zap went through a door and hit Ms James who was taking a lesson with the little kids. She immediately began to unwrite the blackboard at speed. Her chalk flew over the words backwards until the board was completely clean. The little kids gaped. 'Oh no, she's on REWIND,' said Bronson from the front desk.

Pete raced out into the school grounds. The gardener

Tiger (Cameron Nugent) hosts the Spaghetti Pig Out .

was still digging furiously on FAST FORWARD. He was up to his waist in the hole and still going.

Some of the older boys were practising high jump. Pete fired off a quick shot at Gribble who was gaining quickly. It missed, hit a window and bounced off onto a high jumper. He froze in mid jump. Paused like a stationary bird.

Pete saw him and felt guilty. He stopped and hit PLAY. The high jumper collapsed to the ground in a heap. But Pete had lost his lead. Gribble brought him to the ground with a flying tackle.

Rabbit grabbed for the control. 'I've got it, I've got it,' he yelled. He pointed the control at Pete.

'No, no, no,' screamed Pete. A big, smart smile came over Rabbit's face.

'Yes, yes, yes,' he leered. He whipped off a green shot at Pete. Pete pulled out his mirror and deflected it. It hit Rabbit in the head. Rabbit froze solid with a silly grin on his face. Gribble grabbed the control from Rabbit and brought him back to life. The gang raced back into school.

Mr Snapper was being carried out on a stretcher. He lay on his back, still conducting at a furious speed. The librarian tottered onwards, hidden behind her pile of books. She didn't see the deep hole which the gardener had dug himself into. With a scream and a thump the librarian vanished into the hole. Dirt and books flew out in a flurry as the gardener continued to dig.

No one in the school knew what had happened. After a couple of hours everyone went back to normal. Pete didn't say anything. Neither did the gang.

They all went home that afternoon with only one thing on their minds. The Great Spaghetti Pig Out, to be held the next day.

'You can't go through with it,' said Linda. She looked at Pete who was lying on his bed looking at the ceiling.

TALKING BACKWARDS

The idea for the story 'Spaghetti Pig Out' came about in an unusual way. A publisher sent me a newspaper clipping about a scientist who said that one day time would run backwards. Everything that had ever happened in the world would unhappen. It was a very strong idea.

But there were problems. In a world running backwards the smoke would come down the chimney and the fire would unburn. You would pick up the logs and walk out backwards with them. The water would go back into the tap. You would uneat your meal. Kids have written and suggested even worse things which you would do backwards. Anyway, I couldn't write the story because everyone in a backwards world would talk backwards. It wouldn't make sense.

Six months later I bought a video player. I pointed the remote control at the TV and put the video on rewind. Then I pointed it at the cat and put him on rewind. It didn't work on the cat of course. But at that moment 'Spaghetti Pig Out' was born. I could make things go backwards.

I pointed the video control at the cat and pressed REWIND.

Outside, far below the lighthouse, waves crashed on the lonely cliffs.

'Why can't I go through with it?' said Pete.

'Firstly because I'm going to picket the disgusting display and secondly because of what Rabbit is going to do with that control. You'll get ten bowls of spaghetti eaten, and then, kerpow. Rewind. In front of the whole school.'

'Oh no,' said Pete. Not rewind. Yuck. Embarrassing. And Fiona will be there too.'

'Give up,' said Linda. 'Just because you got one kiss doesn't mean she's in love with you.'

Pete went red in the face. He wished that tomorrow would never come. But it did.

The whole hall was packed with kids, parents and teachers. A large banner saying First Annual Spaghetti Pig Out was draped across the stage. A long queue of kids waited to get in. Linda walked up and down holding signs saying Only Pigs Pig Out.

Near the front Mr Snapper sat next to Ms James on a bench seat. Dad edged his way towards a very small space between them. He wriggled awkwardly into the gap. Ms James shifted sideways to try and make room. Mr Snapper glared at Dad.

Dad smiled at Ms James. His blood pressure went up from just thinking about her. 'Er, look, about the other day, Fay,' he began. 'It's not what you think. I didn't mean to pull down my pants. Something came over me.'

Mr Snapper's eyes widened. 'I'll bet it did,' he said.

Mr Gribble and Matron Gribble who were in the front row, turned around and looked at Dad with disgust.

'No, no, it's not like that,' said poor Dad. 'Something funny happened. Can't explain it.'

Ms James smiled a friendly smile. 'You've got nice legs anyway,' she said.

STORYBOARDS

When a director receives the final draft of a script, he gets together with an artist and produces a storyboard. It shows what will be in every shot to be made by the cameras. These are not left until the last minute but carefully worked out in advance. Here is the storyboard for the last scene in 'Spaghetti Pig Out':

▶

Suddenly there was a fanfare from the stage. Tiger walked through the curtains wearing a loud, checked outfit. Kids started cheering and booing as he picked up the microphone. He held up his hands. 'Thank you, thank you, fans. Welcome to the First Annual Spaghetti Pig Out. As you know, the prize is a ten-speed bike.'

Jill Henderson, dressed in a silky gown, wheeled out the bike and draped herself around Tiger. Cheers went up from the hall.

'And now,' said Tiger with a flourish, 'let me hear it for our valiant competitors.'

The crowd cheered and jeered as the curtain swished aside. There, on the stage, behind a long table, sat Pete, Rabbit, Bessie and Tanya. Each had a fork in front of them. To one side was another table laden with scores of bowls of steaming spaghetti bolognaise.

'Our first competitor,' yelled Tiger. 'Is the skinny, but ever-hungry, Termite Twist.' The crowd cheered. A few booed. Dad smiled at Ms James.

Pete sat there nervously. He wished he was home in bed. He felt ill. Fiona was in the front row watching. He wondered what she was thinking. His coach, Bronson, stood behind dressed in a white robe. He had a towel around his neck.

Tiger moved on to the next seat. 'Let's hear it for Rabbit the Ravisher.' Cheers and boos from the audience. Rabbit thumped one hand into the other. He wore a black dressing-gown. Gribble massaged Rabbit's cheeks. They both grinned confidently.

Tiger turned to another contestant. 'In the far seat is the firm favourite, Bessie the Bottomless Pit.' Everyone cheered wildly. All the bets were on Bessie. She popped a boiled lolly into her mouth and sucked it noisily.

This only left a thin, tall girl. 'And last, but not least,' said Tiger, 'Tapeworm Tania.' More cheers. Tania smiled modestly.

115

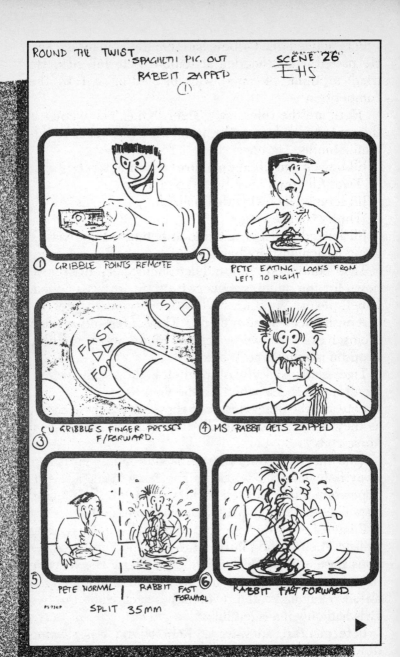

ROUND THE TWIST   SPAGHETTI PIC. OUT   SCENE 26
                   RABBIT ZAPPED   EHS
                        (1)

① GRIBBLE POINTS REMOTE

② PETE EATING. LOOKS FROM LEFT TO RIGHT

③ CU GRIBBLES FINGER PRESSES F/FORWARD.

④ MS RABBIT GETS ZAPPED

⑤ PETE NORMAL | RABBIT FAST FORWARD
       SPLIT 35mm

⑥ RABBIT FAST FORWARD.

PS·7269

Pete noticed that Gribble had something in his pocket. He patted it and nodded at Rabbit. Pete felt sick. He tried to think of some way of getting out of the competition.

'Here are the rules,' said Tiger. 'One. The winner is the contestant who eats the most bowls of spaghetti in fifteen minutes.'

Jill bowed and lifted up a bowl for all to see.

'Two. All bowls must be scraped clean.'

Jill scraped a bowl with a flourish.

'Three. No spewing.'

Jill looked at Tiger and shook her head. She wasn't going to demonstrate being sick for anyone.

Tiger continued. 'All candidates must keep their meal down for ten minutes. Otherwise they are disqualified. Quiet, please. We can't start until everyone is quiet.'

A hush fell over the audience. The contestants readied themselves. Lips were licked. Forks were fondled. Bronson mopped Pete's brow.

Tiger held up a fistful of spaghetti. 'Get set,' he yelled. He dropped the spaghetti to the floor. 'Go.'

Pete and the others began to shovel in spaghetti as fast as they could go. Tiger called the action as if it was a horse race.

'And they're eating. Bessie the Bottomless Pit is first away followed by Ravishing Rabbit and Termite Twist. Tapeworm Tania faltered at the barrier but is closing in fast. The field is equal at two bowls each.'

Fingers flew as the four contestants went into a feeding frenzy. They pushed in the steaming food at a tremendous pace. Arms whirled like propellers. For a while they were all close but gradually Pete and Rabbit edged ahead. They had eaten seven bowls each while the two girls had only managed five.

Pete glanced sideways at Rabbit who was slowing down. Gribble fondled a bulge in his back pocket.

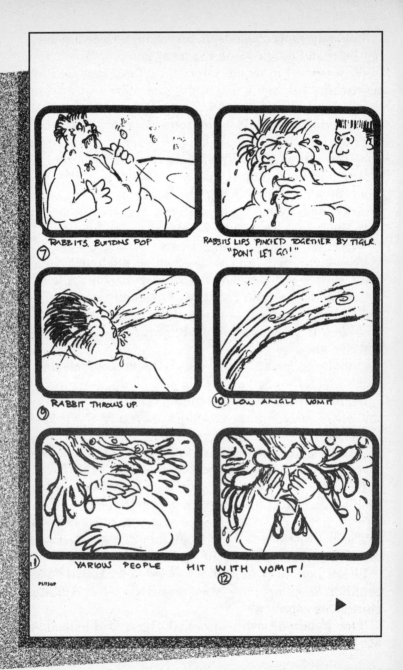

⑦ RABBITS. BUTTONS POP

RABBITS LIPS PINCHED TOGETHER BY TIGER.
"DONT LET GO!"

⑨ RABBIT THROWS UP.

⑩ LOW ANGLE VOMIT

⑪ VARIOUS PEOPLE

HIT WITH VOMIT!

⑫

Suddenly Tania conked out. She slumped face first into her bowl and gurgled into the meat sauce.

Tiger moved in for an interview. 'Tania is gone,' he screamed. 'Yes, she's definitely gone. She's thrown in the fork at seven bowls. What a woman. Tania, what happened? You were odds on for a place.'

Tania raised her bloated face. 'I don't know,' she gurgled. 'I ate seventeen plates at practice this morning.'

Pete and Rabbit continued to gobble. Pete edged in front by one plate. Suddenly Bessie stood up. She groaned and moaned. She tottered and then tumbled onto the floor, clutching her stomach.

'Stretcher bearers,' yelled Tiger.

Bessie was carried off while Pete and Rabbit fed on. The score grew to fifteeen-thirteen with Pete in the lead.

Gribble had moved to the front row of the hall. He took out the control. Pete's heart sank. He was gone. Gribble was going to put him on REWIND in front of Fiona and the whole school.

Gribble pointed the control. At Rabbit. Rabbit nodded. Gribble grinned. And pressed FAST FORWARD.

A green spark zapped Rabbit's chest. He began to shovel the spaghetti at enormous speed. His fork flew like a whirlwind. His arms moved so quickly that they were only a blur. No one had ever eaten that fast before. Twenty bowls. Thirty bowls. Sixty bowls.

The crowd fell silent. They couldn't believe it. Mr Gribble sprang to his feet. 'That's my boy,' he yelled. 'He's signed with me.'

The hall broke into pandemonium. Kids yelled and cheered. Others grew afraid.

Jill rushed out with the bowls of spaghetti. She couldn't keep up with the furious pace of Rabbit's gluttonous gobbling.

'One hundred bowls,' shrieked Tiger. Dad looked at Ms James in horror.

⑬ GRIBBLE STUMBLES BACK WITH REMOTE CONTROL AS VOMIT HITS

⑭ RABBIT SETTLES.

⑮ TRACK ALONG VOMIT COVERED AUDIENCE

⑯ GRIBBLE IN VOMIT POOL HOLDING UP REMOTE CONTROL

⑰ GRIBBLE IN VOMIT POOL PETES FEET STEP IN, HAND GRABS REMOTE CONTROL → TILT UP

⑱ END OF TILT

120

Pete wearily and slowly pushed spaghetti into his mouth. Nineteen bowls. He couldn't keep up. No one could match Rabbit's mad mastications.

'This is a personal best for Rabbit,' yelled Tiger. 'No, more than that. A national record. An international record. Australia is showing the world how it's done.'

The clock showed thirty seconds to go. Rabbit was still going. He grew enormous. With every forkful he expanded. He was elephant sized. His buttons popped. His belt snapped. And still he sucked and swallowed spaghetti.

The siren sounded. It was all over. Pete slumped in his chair, defeated. But Rabbit ate on and on. Gribble was mesmerised. He had forgotten about the control. Suddenly he remembered and zapped the gigantic Rabbit.

Tiger held up Rabbit's arm. 'The winner is Rabbit the Ravishing Ratbag,' he yelled. 'No, wait. Something is amiss. I fear the worst. Rabbit is not well. Rabbit is fed up.'

There were cheers and boos from the audience. People moved nervously in their seats. Rabbit tottered towards the edge of the stage. His face was green. His cheeks were bloated. His stomach rumbled terribly. He stared down at Gribble who looked up with terrified eyes.

Gribble rushed up and pinned Rabbit's lips together with his fingers. 'Keep it in. Keep it in,' he screamed. 'You can do it. Swallow. Look at the horizon. Don't let go.'

Mr Gribble, Matron Gribble, Fiona and the others in the front row stared up in fear. They threw up their hands across their faces. 'Keep it down, boy. Keep it down,' yelled Matron Gribble.

Mr Gribble was filled with panic. 'James, hold those lips,' he ordered. 'Think of your mother.'

'An upset. A belly big upset,' shouted Tiger. He held

the microphone to Rabbit's stomach. The gurgling was louder than a thousand baths emptying at the same time.

Rabbit wobbled on the edge of the stage. His eyes bulged. His lips slipped out of Gribble's fingers. His mouth opened.

He spewed. He spouted. He threw up all over Gribble. All over the front three rows. A waterfall. A river of puked pasta. Gribble was washed off the stage in the terrible flood.

The audience shrieked. They threw up their arms. They panicked and ran for the door. But for the front three rows there was no escape. They sat motionless. White eyes blinked through the covering of vomited spaghetti bolognaise.

Gribble was buried. A squirming, worm-covered figure on the floor.

Pete was piled with it. Linda was lost in it. Bronson was buried in it. Dozens of others dripped with it.

Pete wiped his eyes. He looked at the buried Gribble. A spaghetti-covered hand stuck out of the goo. Pete bent down and picked up the control.

He pointed it at Rabbit.

'No, no, no,' shrieked Rabbit.

'Yes, yes, yes,' chorused Pete, Bronson and Linda.

Pete's finger pressed the REWIND button.

Wrap

When they are shooting a film nobody is allowed to go home until the director shouts 'Wrap', at the end of each day. When he does, everyone leaves. Fast.

When a film is finally finished the cast and crew hold a Wrap Party. It's a big occasion. The next day everyone will leave for new jobs. Or go home with no job. Some will meet again. Some will never meet again. Presents are given. Tears are cried. Farewells are spoken. It's a wild night. Everyone has worked so hard and now it's all over. That's it.

And that's it for this book. It's 'Wrap'. I hope you've enjoyed it (and the TV series which has many more stories than I have included here).

How do I feel now that Round the Twist is finished? Very happy. Very sad. I met some wonderful people. Had some great laughs. Like everyone else involved, I slaved my guts out.

I'm off to Sydney next week. That's where Esben lives. I think I might call in at his place. All the news is good, but just the same, I might take him some Danish pastry. This bit will taste really sweet.

QUIRKY TAILS

A Santa Claws, a sneeze'n coffin, a train full of terrible roses, ghosts for hire, stuffed (and not so stuffed) toads, a copying machine with a difference and more. Here are nine more ingenious stories – each bizarre and each with a twist in the tail.

THE CABBAGE PATCH FIB

I watched as Chris put the baby on the ground and started to creep off. 'What are you doing?' I shouted. 'You can't go off and leave it.'

'It's not mine,' he yelled back. 'I don't want it. This is where it came from and I'm putting it back.' Without another word he turned and rushed off. His footsteps faded into the night.

I looked at the baby. It was already turning purple and had stopped breathing. I didn't know what to do . . .

THE SILK AND THE SKIN
Rodie Sudbery

What are Ralph and his gang always doing in the churchyard? Guy just *has* to find out, although it's obvious they're up to no good. He soon discovers that he and his backward younger brother are being drawn into a nightmarish situation – but where is Guy going to find the courage to stand up against Ralph and his gang – and the forces of the supernatural they've already summoned . . .?

FINN MAC COOL AND THE SMALL MEN OF DEEDS
Pat O'Shea

Finn Mac Cool is the bravest, wisest, tallest and rudest of the warriors of the Fianna. Unfortunately, when the giant arrives to ask for his help Finn just happens to have a very bad headache. He is the only hope for saving the heir to the throne in the country of the giants so Gariv, the sly old servant, has to use all his wiles to get Finn on his feet and ready for battle.

RACE AGAINST TIME
Rosemary Hayes

From the moment Livvy sees the island, she knows there is something wrong. A strange and menacing force beckons, drawing her and her brother into a race against time. They are destined to fulfil an ancient quest to restore a magical cross to its rightful owner, but they must face the forces of unparalleled evil to do so.

ROSCOE'S LEAP

Gillian Cross

To Hannah, living in a weird and fantastical old house means endlessly having to fix things like heating systems and furnaces, but for Stephen it is a place where something once happened to him, something dark and terrifying which he doesn't want to remember but cannot quite forget. Then a stranger intrudes upon the family and asks questions about the past that force Hannah to turn her attention from mechanical things to human feelings, and drive Stephen to meet the terror that is locked away inside him, waiting . . .

OVER THE MOON AND FAR AWAY

Margaret Nash

The new girl at school calls herself a 'traveller' and says she comes from beyond the stars. Ben doesn't believe her, of course, but then again Zillah isn't quite like anyone he and his friends have ever met. There's her name for a start, and she doesn't even know how to play their games. But the mysterious new-comer does seem able to make things happen . . .

THE TROUBLE WITH JACOB

Eloise McGraw

Right from the start there is something very weird about the boy Andy sees on the hillside. Every time Andy's twin sister Kat is there he just disappears, and all he ever talks about is his bed! Andy thinks he's going mad, but then he and Kat decide that someone is playing tricks on them. There must be some logical solution to the mystery. After all, the only other explanation would be far too incredible . . .